STONES

SIAN B. CLAVEN

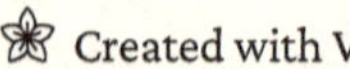 Created with Vellum

This book is dedicated to Sam, Toni, and Jackie. Without your support, I would never write anything good.

ACKNOWLEDGMENTS

There are always so many people that I want to thank for contributing to my writing process.

I cannot miss mentioning the incredible support I receive from my sister, who is an avid fan and my best reviewer. I know I'm on the right track if she enjoys the story.

Without Toni, I would be a mess. She is my rock and my sounding board, and I'm lucky to have her. Not to mention she proofs my books like a champ.

Sam is just a superstar, helping me plot (especially books I have yet to write), and is an amazing editor who makes my books shine.

A special shout out to Ashleigh and Tamsyn, who both always care so deeply about me and my writing, and because you can message Ashleigh anytime you're stuck, and she'll help you.

To my ARC team, I appreciate you so much. I would be nothing without you.

To my fans, I hope you enjoy this book. It certainly had its moments where I was crying. I hope you can forgive me once you're done.

CHAPTER 1

2016 - 17 Years Old

HE WOKE UP BEFORE DAWN. THE SMALL ALARM CLOCK ON HIS bedside table rang loudly to get him up. He flipped his blanket off of his body, got up, and promptly made his bed. Once done, he went to the bathroom to have a hot shower; he didn't know how long he was going out for this time and didn't know the next time he would see a shower.

He wanted to indulge and have a long, hot shower and let the heat really soak into his bones, but Father was already awake and downstairs and would not tolerate tardiness.

Switching the shower off, Hunter wrapped a towel around his waist and brushed his teeth before going back to his room to dry and dress. Discarding the towel in his hamper, he dressed warmly in his hunting camouflage and pulled on the matching cap to hide his blond semi-dry hair.

A breakfast of sausages and eggs was already on the table, steam rising from the plate. Father set down two cups of coffee as Hunter reached the bottom of the stairs. Father looked up at him without a smile and nodded for him to sit himself down.

Hunter pulled out a chair and took his place at the table. Not a word passed between them. Father preferred quiet reflections in the morning, so not even the radio was switched on.

They ate in silence.

Once Hunter had finished washing the dishes, with no sign of dawn yet, Father handed him a camping bag, a tent, and a rifle. Hunter knew and trusted that Father would pack everything he needed in the bag; there was no reason to check it.

They left.

Father drove him away from their cabin in the woods and further into the forest than where they lived, and they already lived deep in nature. The crunch of the leaves under the truck's wheels was all they heard for quite some time before the sound of rushing water rose in volume.

Hunter wasn't sure which part of the forest they were in; they'd been traveling for so long the sun was beginning to rise. As it did, the forest around them stirred. Creatures darted between the trees as the truck crunched its way through. They stopped near a river, and Father looked forward.

"I haven't decided when I'll be back." He didn't look at Hunter, and Hunter didn't say anything as he climbed out of the truck and retrieved his goods.

The truck reversed and disappeared from view. Hunter didn't stand around to watch it go off; he needed to spring into action immediately.

He walked through the trees, keeping an eye out for a suitable area to camp. He found a small flat space, not far from the river but far enough so the wind blowing off the water wouldn't chill him at night.

He set up his tent in front of a tree and dug and built a fire pit using a small hand shovel from his pack and rocks he collected from the river.

He filled his water canteen while by the water before bringing the stones back and stacking them up around the hole he had made.

Before he could go hunt, he needed wood. He kept his hunting knife strapped to his leg just in case and held his rifle slung over his shoulder as he collected as much wood as he could carry, not once but three times. He had a stack of wood that would last throughout the night once he made his fire.

Now was the time to find food. Hunter knew there was none in the pack Father had handed him. This was a test of his survival skills, and he had to prove he was a man.

He picked up his rifle and pocketed some extra ammo before moving away from his campsite and into the forest, where he was sure to find rabbits or deer. He made a rough hideout of some bushes and hunkered down, waiting.

After an hour of silence, some bushes nearby rustled, and he trained his gun on them. A rabbit hopped out of the thicket of leaves. It was a large rabbit, lots of meat on the bones. It would do perfectly.

Hunter took aim, and once the rabbit was still enough, he fired, hitting it. The creature fell to the ground, twitching slightly. Hunter removed himself from his makeshift hide and walked over to his kill, unsheathing his knife and slitting its throat.

He didn't need more; if he were here longer, he would hunt again, but this rabbit was enough for now. He grabbed it by its ears and walked back the way he had come. He found his campsite easily and hung the rabbit in a tree nearby, away from other predators.

The forest was alive now with the noise of nature, and Hunter felt calm. Yes, there were bears in the woods, and if you went close to the mountains, certain big cats could attack you, but none of these frightened him. You handled a situation when it became a situation.

Hunter put the wood in his pit and sourced his lighter to get the fire going. He would skin the rabbit in the meantime and make a stand for a skewer so he could roast the rabbit over the open flames.

He worked on the rabbit diligently. Looking up at the occasional rustle of leaves or bushes, but he was mostly given a wide berth. Until he heard what was unmistakably footsteps in the brush. He hung the bits of rabbit back up in the tree and grabbed his rifle, heading in the direction he had heard the noise.

A deer darted in front of him, but he wasn't startled. He lifted his rifle and scanned the area.

"Hey," someone whispered, and he looked a few yards away, "I'm tracking that deer."

Hunter nodded and lowered his gun, turning around to leave.

"You can help," the older man said as he got closer. "My name's Kane."

He held out his hand, and Hunter shook it, keeping his eyes focused on Kane's face until he shifted uncomfortably.

"You can go around to the south, and I'll approach from the north. I'll take first shot, and if I miss, you can follow up as she comes down to you, okay?"

Hunter nodded and turned to go north. He didn't look back at Kane but noticed he did walk heavily for a hunter. Hunter waited a moment and then turned around and quietly followed Kane.

He wanted first shot.

Kane found a good spot upwind from the deer and

laid down, propping his rifle on a log and aiming for the deer. He didn't even hear Hunter approach him from behind. Hunter raised his rifle, and before Kane could take his shot, Hunter pulled the trigger, shooting the man in the head.

Kane slumped forward, and Hunter smiled to himself. He admired the perfect shot, even though it was close range, and then picked up Kane's rifle and slung it over his shoulder.

He grabbed Kane by the arms and started to drag him back toward the campsite. It took a lot of effort and a few hours to get there, but as the sun set, Hunter reached the site.

It looked like some animals had gotten brave and poked around. He checked that the rabbit was untouched, and once he was sure it was fine, Hunter pulled Kane's body next to the fire pit.

Hunter got the fire going again and warmed himself before taking some long swigs of water. He got up and filled his canteen before coming back. Flies buzzed around Kane's body. Hunter shooed them away and took out his hunting knife, stabbing it into the ground next to the body.

He undressed Kane, his hands trembling slightly in excitement. It was a bit difficult to get the clothes off, and eventually, Hunter used his knife to slice through the little that was left, tearing them off.

He used the light of the fire, and the moon in the

clear sky above, to inspect the body. Kane had been an average man with a beer belly and small dick. Nothing to write home about.

But Hunter could practice.

Using the hunting knife, Hunter started to cut open Kane's body. From shoulder to chest, from the other shoulder to chest, and then down the abdomen. He cut deep into the tissue and then managed to open the incision up.

Blood covered his hands and the ground around them. It had a metallic stink to it, but Hunter wasn't bothered by it; it wasn't the first time he'd had blood on his hands. He was used to being surrounded by death.

He poked around in Kane's abdomen, lifting the organs as far as he could in his hands and letting them slip back. He wanted to memorize the texture of them, the shape of them, everything about them. Most of all, he wanted to crack open Kane's chest and squeeze his heart until it popped.

But he was hungry now. Leaving Kane's body where it was, Hunter got up, rinsed his hands, and got the rabbit. He skewered it on a sharpened stick and rested it on two stands he'd made from sticks and string he found in his pack.

While that roasted, with him turning it every now and then, he knelt back by Kane's body. He realized he wouldn't have the strength and didn't have the tools to crack open the man's chest to reach his heart, so he'd have to go from the bottom.

Hunter gleefully yanked out the organs, slicing them with his hunting knife and setting them in a pile beside him, until Kane's body was devoid of organs and Hunter could start yanking the lungs down through the abdomen.

It was difficult because he had to get both hands in there to cut the connecting tissue. But he managed to do it, and soon, he triumphantly held Kane's heart in his hand.

Hunter stared at it as the blood, congealing, dripped down his arm. He squeezed the heart; it was tough, and he knew he wouldn't be able to 'pop' it the way he wanted to. He dug his nails into it and then dug the nails of his other hand into it and tried to tear it. Some of the muscles tore, but it was a resilient thing.

After washing the man's blood off his hands, again, he took the rabbit off the fire, and using another stick, he skewered the heart and put it over the fire. He let the roasted rabbit cool while the heart was cooked. It was exciting, the thoughts flying through his mind, about how he had rid the world of Kane.

As soon as the rabbit was cool enough, he cut pieces of it off and ate it, saving most of it for the morning. Once the heart was ready, he took it off the flames and set it down to cool on a rock. It was late; the moon was high in the sky, but adrenaline coursed through his veins. He wasn't tired in the least.

As soon as he could, he picked up the heart, removed it from the stick, and lifted it to his face. He inhaled the cooked muscle and sighed before taking a slow, calculated bite of the flesh.

He could feel energy coursing through his veins, and he knew this was something that would make Father proud. He would discard the rest of Kane near bear territory to be feasted on. But the heart was his.

Once he had consumed the last bite, he took a walk to the river, and even in the cold night air, he stripped down and waded in, unafraid of what may lurk in the water. He feared nothing.

He washed the rest of the blood off himself and climbed out of the water. He sat in the dark, goosebumps forming on his skin and his dick shriveling up because of the cool air. He waited awhile, gathered his things, and went back to his campsite to dry himself by the fire and dress.

In the morning, he was surprised to hear the crunching of leaves. It sounded like something heavy was coming through the forest.

He jumped up and grabbed his rifle, exiting his tent quickly. He saw Father's truck creeping through the forest and was taken aback. Father normally gave him three or four days in the woods; he never came back so early to collect him.

Father stopped the truck and climbed out, coming to the makeshift campsite and looking down at Kane.

"It was foolish but admirable," Father said. "We must get rid of the body now. People are looking for him. I knew you were involved."

Hunter lowered his head in respect. "Do I apologize?"

"Are you sorry?" Father asked.

"No," Hunter said simply, looking back up at Father.

"Then you don't apologize; come. Pack up and load the body." Father went to sit in the warm truck while Hunter cleaned up his mess. Father didn't even get out to help him when the teenager struggled slightly to lift Kane into the bed of the truck.

It was Hunter's mess. He had to clean it. This was his lesson.

Once he was done, he climbed into the front of the truck and rested his rifle between them, next to Father's rifle.

"Well done," Father said, but there was no trace of a smile on his face, and he didn't sound proud. He was simply stating a fact. "You're almost ready."

Hunter nodded and turned to face forward, not saying another word while they traveled through the forest. Not when they disposed of Kane's body and not when they got back to the cabin.

Hunter was surprised to see another truck parked outside of the cabin. In all the years they'd lived here, no one had visited, so he stopped when he climbed out of the truck, apprehensive.

"No one is here," Father said calmly. "The truck is yours. A gift. You need to learn to drive to be ready."

Hunter touched the truck lightly and nodded. "Thank you for this gift, Father."

"Go clean your clothes and prepare breakfast. I'm going to get supplies." Father climbed back into his truck and backed out.

Hunter did as he was told.

2021 - PRESENT DAY

January - Donovan

Donovan could feel warm kisses on his neck, and he murmured his approval. Still in bed, he was sleepy but satisfied. He knew the kisses were from Sam, his wife, and he slowly opened his eyes to her naked form lying next to him in bed.

"Hello, what's this?" he asked gleefully.

Sam grinned. "Birthday kafoofaling before the kids get up," Sam murmured in reply.

They kissed deeply and made passionate, although rather quick love, and soon they were both spent, relaxing in each other's arms. Sam's head rested on Donovan's chest.

"What's for lunch since we've had breakfast?"

Donovan teased, and Sam chuckled; she loved her husband's sense of humor.

"We had better get up before the kids come barging in." Sam sat up, reaching for the robe she had discarded to the floor. Donovan also got up and walked to their en-suite bathroom to shower.

Sam wanted to join him but knew their preteen son and young daughter would be up and hungry soon. Besides, it was Saturday and Donovan's birthday. He should get to enjoy a hot shower without interruptions, no matter how sexy. She left him to his own devices while she got dressed and went downstairs to see to their children.

Donovan stood under the hot shower, satisfied and happy. It was a great way to start a birthday, and since it was still early, he might be able to get in a hike before the family wanted to do something together.

Hikes were mainly Donovan's thing, and the family knew that. It was how he de-stressed from the week of being the CEO of his own IT technical support company.

The company had grown exponentially the last year, so much so they had been able to afford a new, larger house and the best schooling for their son Ollie and their daughter Valentina.

It was stressful, but hiking alone calmed Donovan and helped him keep his laidback composure. And since the family didn't want for anything, monetarily or emotionally, they indulged his need for his alone time.

Donovan was, however, very hungry after his morning tryst with Sam, so he finished showering, got dry and dressed, and walked downstairs to the kitchen, where everyone was seated at the island in the center of the room.

"Good morning, darling," Sam said, kissing his cheek. She handed him a plate of his favorite choc-chip flapjacks, and he sat at the head of the island.

"Morning, Daddy."

"Morning, Dad."

He smiled. "Morning, kiddos."

They got up and came to hug him tightly. "Happy birthday," they chorused.

"Mommy, can we give Daddy his presents now?" Val asked.

Sam looked at Donovan, and he nodded. "Sure, I'd love to have some presents now, but only pick one each."

They had piled the presents by the fireplace as they bought them, and Donovan had a sizeable pile, always spoiled rotten by Sam and through her, the kids.

They came running back, each with a box in hand.

"That was quick. It's almost as though you knew exactly which ones to get me." He smiled. "Hmmm, I wonder what these could be."

He first took the box from Ollie and opened it painstakingly slowly until the children were begging him to go faster. He laughed and ripped the paper off the box, and smiled brightly.

"New hiking boots!" he declared happily. "This will be so useful for my hike in a bit. Thank you, Ollie." He leaned down and kissed the top of his son's head.

Val held out her box, and Donovan ripped the paper off and chuckled, "How did you fit this hiking backpack in this box?"

Val grinned. "Mommy did it."

"It's deception," Donovan declared, leaning down to kiss his daughter. "Thank you, sweetheart. I'm going to have breakfast and then go for my hike, and I think afterward we can all go bowling."

The kids cheered, and Sam ushered them back to their seats to finish their breakfast. Sam set a small box down next to Donovan's plate. "And this is from Mommy."

Donovan smiled and opened the box; he kissed Sam suddenly and deeply, and when he broke the kiss, he gave her a happy grin. "Thank you, baby. I really needed a new fitness watch to count my steps. I'm going for a personal record this year."

"Well, it's January, so the perfect time to start." Sam sat down at the other end of the island, and they finished their breakfast, conversing about bowling later and what the family would be doing while Donovan was hiking.

Soon he was getting his new gear ready and trying on his new hiking boots, which fit perfectly, and he was ready to go.

He kissed both the kids and then gave Sam a long, slow kiss. "I'll only hike for like an hour, half an hour up and half an hour down, then I'll come back so we can celebrate," he promised.

"Enjoy it, baby. We love you so much."

"I love you guys too," Donovan replied, leaving the house.

He climbed into his car and blasted a host of old rock songs while he drove out of suburbia and toward the national park that he loved to hike in. There were a lot of great trails in the park, but Donovan knew which one he wanted to do today. He wanted that view of the city by the cliffside that no one ever went to because it was a hard trail. It would be a challenge to do it in half an hour there, but he knew he could; he'd been hiking for years.

He parked in the designated parking spot and was pleased to see there weren't many cars yet. The first two weeks of January, the place had been overrun as people decided to exercise more for their New Year's resolutions, but it had died down now evidently; people were predictable.

Donovan slung his backpack over his shoulder and took his walking cane, and walked to the start of the trail. Taking even, measured breaths, he started his ascent up the trail, not stopping because he didn't want to break his rhythm.

As he walked, he thought about the various things that irked him at work that week and just let them go, letting the adrenaline from the hike kill off the bad vibes he had had.

Twenty minutes in and without stopping, Donovan pulled his water bottle from his bag and took a mighty sip. His legs were starting to cramp, but he knew he could make it to the top with a few minutes to spare if he just pushed on.

He kept a hold of his water bottle as he walked, sipping from it periodically, and although his gait was somewhat slower, he did make it to the top of the cliff in twenty-eight minutes, a personal record.

He beamed with pride as he stood on the edge of the cliff, overlooking the vast forest and the city that lay beyond it. To the left, the forest continued to expand, and there were certain markers, Donovan had seen them, that warned not to go in past a certain distance or you could get lost or attacked by wild animals.

Donovan contemplated bringing the kids camping in the national park; they would love to do that. Maybe he would even take them hiking with him and spend some quality time with them. Lord knew that he needed a vacation, and what better way to spend your day than hiking through nature.

Suddenly the cliff by his feet exploded as though something hard had hit it, and Donovan jumped, misplaced his footing, and slid down the cliff. He tried to grab the edge, but the edge was too rounded to cling to.

Suddenly he was free-falling so fast, and then it

ended—it took both a long time to hit the ground and almost no time at all, and the wind was knocked out of Donovan. The crack of his ankle caused him to scream out in pain once he caught his breath.

He screamed a few times before taking a few deep breaths and looking up at the cliff. "Can someone help me, please?" he called. "Can anyone hear me?"

He continued to call out between groans and was startled when he heard leaves crunching near him. He looked around, worried that a wild animal was nearby. He kept quiet, not wanting to draw it to him.

Then he saw a hunter emerge from some bushes; he had his rifle in his hand and looked at Donovan curiously.

"Please, sir, I fell down the cliff. Please, I need you to get help or help me to the medical center."

The hunter nodded and shouldered his gun before going to Donovan and offering his hands. With some maneuvering, Donovan managed to get up.

He tried to put weight on the broken ankle, but his leg was having none of that. He leaned on the hunter, and they limped/hopped their way through the forest, the hunter leading the way. He didn't say anything, though, and it made Donovan nervous.

"I'm Donovan, by the way. Thank you for coming to my rescue."

The hunter nodded, and they approached a clearing where a truck was parked. Donovan sighed with relief, and then a large brown mass caught his attention. A large bear was lying, dead, in the bed of the truck.

"Er, those are endangered, aren't they? Not that I would tell anyone after what you've done for me."

The hunter didn't respond and instead helped Donovan onto the back of the truck, next to the bear. Donovan grimaced but didn't complain. "It makes sense for me to sit with my leg straight; don't want to put weight on it, good thinking."

The hunter closed the back of the truck and walked around it. Donovan settled down; the dull throbbing of his ankle was getting worse, and where he had scraped and cut himself on the rocks was burning. He knew Sam was going to be pissed because she'd told him to stay away from the cliffs.

There was a click, and then everything was gone.

HUNTER

Donovan spoke too much, and Hunter really didn't care for what he had to say. After he had shot the rocks near Donovan's feet, he had been most pleased that Donovan had fallen down the cliff as planned. When Donovan initially arrived, Hunter hadn't known which trail he would pick and was glad he chose the least popular one.

Hunting him had been easy.

Hopefully, Father would approve of this one; after all, Hunter had learned a lot and was now twenty-one. He felt he was ready, but only Father could say so.

Hunter got into his truck and made his way through the forest, deeper and deeper. He and Father had long ago made their own markings for how to drive through the trees without getting stuck, and they knew the forest better than anyone. Hunter drove in quiet contentment for an hour and a half before he saw their cabin up ahead.

Next to a small lake, their cabin was hidden on all sides by large bushes. It was a carefully chosen area, and the construction of the cabin had taken Father years, long before Hunter was born. He pulled up to his parking spot and stopped the truck.

First things first, he opened up the back of the truck, pulled Donovan's lifeless body toward him, and threw Donovan over his shoulder like a sack of potatoes.

Hunter carried Donovan as though he weighed nothing, but Hunter had trained and prepared to move large weights his whole life.

He carried the body into the cabin, and to the left, he went down some stairs to the basement. It was a sterile room, cordoned off by plastic. In the center of the room was a gurney, instruments lined the wall, and on a counter near the gurney was a large, polished wooden box a yard long and a few inches wide.

Hunter carefully lowered Donovan onto the gurney

and left him there; the room was temperature-controlled, and he couldn't do anything until both Father said so and rigor mortis had passed.

Hunter instead went to get the bear off the truck. He used the mounted pulley on the back to get it off, just as he had used it to get the damn thing on.

Once on the ground, Hunter got his knives, donned overalls, and set to work gutting, skinning, and preparing the bear.

It was hours' worth of work, and it was past lunch by the time he was done. But he was finished, the meat was stored, and the hide was ready to be treated by Father.

Hunter went inside and showered before washing his clothes and making a sandwich. He sat at the small square table in one of the two chairs and turned the radio on to a music channel that played classical music while he ate. He sometimes appreciated the music in the background, but Hunter preferred peace and quiet overall. Especially when he was studying. Father had home-schooled him and taught him everything he knew from skinning, cooking, survival, biology and chemistry and math, and med school things like autopsies. Who needed the modern world's way of teaching; Hunter was adept at it all without their ways.

And Father had taught him the most important lesson of all. Humans are worthless; they have forgotten that it's survival of the fittest, and it was Hunter and Father's job to remind them of that.

Cops were their worst enemy because they would try and get in the way, but Father had studied the greatest of their craft—cops called it serial killing. Hunter called it culling out the weak. Nonetheless, they would never be stopped.

The sound of tires brought him out of his thoughts. His sandwich was finished. He shut off the radio and washed his plate before dusting himself off, running a hand through his hair, and walking to the door.

Father's truck was next to Hunter's, and he could see Father had caught a large stag for dinner. Father would skin it himself; whoever shot it skinned it. That was Father's way.

The first animal Hunter had shot had been the dog his Father had given him as a gift. He had raised it, cared for it, and then Father had told him to kill it because there was no place in the world for the weak. Hunter had skinned the dog, eaten the meat, treated the hide, and made a rug for his room.

Father stepped out of his vehicle, bringing Hunter out of this thoughts once more. It was his greatest fault, getting lost in his own mind. Father deplored it, but he had to show Father he was present.

Father walked to the house and past Hunter, heading downstairs. There was absolute silence for the longest time, and Hunter did his best not to let his thoughts wander off. Suddenly he heard footsteps as Father ascended the stairs and came out again, heading to his truck to sort out his stag.

"Come, boy," Father said.

Hunter moved quickly to help Father get the stag off the truck, and once they had it down, he retrieved Father's knives and overalls.

Father started to cut open the stag. "You're ready."

It's all he had to say. Hunter tried not to let his emotions show, although his hands did shake slightly. Father didn't look up, and Hunter turned and left. He went back downstairs and tested the body; he should be able to cut it open now.

He retrieved the various surgeon tools Father had collected over the years and got dressed in surgical scrubs and gloves before making an incision down the front of Donovan's chest, followed by sawing through the bone to crack it open.

He worked with precision to carefully retrieve the heart and place it in a jar that he had set on the counter. He then picked up a cloth to wipe the blood off his hands before opening the wooden box.

In the wooden box were twelve cubes, each with a stone in the center and an engraved plate on the bottom front of the cube. Hunter picked the first one up and went back to Donovan's body, carefully placing the cube where the heart had been before he started to close him up.

Satisfied, he dressed Donovan in everyday clothes you could buy at any franchised supermarket and waited for Father.

Father came downstairs and inspected his work before nodding. "Take him. Do not be seen."

Hunter hauled Donovan upstairs, his dead weight slowing him down a bit, and he put him on the back of the truck. It was almost ten at night, but Hunter knew how to get to the main road that led out of the forest rather easily. It was disused and abandoned, but it did the trick.

He packed a bag of supplies in the truck and headed out, driving toward the pier.

CHAPTER 2

"I'm just saying, we need to discuss being bullied with her; we need to handle this carefully," Lexie told Danny as she put her earrings in.

Danny was busy doing his tie. "Thea is a big girl, Lex. She can take care of herself, I'm sure."

Lexie sighed. "Danny, I'm asking you to handle one thing."

Danny kissed his wife on the cheek. "Okay, I'll speak to her now before school."

He left their bedroom and went across the hall, knocking softly on the blue door.

"Come in," Thea called; his fifteen-year-old daughter was sitting on her bed as he opened the door.

"Hey, sweetheart," Danny smiled, "Mom tells me you're getting bullied at school."

Thea looked up at him, her eyes wide. "I told her not to say anything."

"It's no big deal. I'm not going to make it a big deal," Danny held his hands up, crossing the room and sitting on the bed opposite her, "I just want you to know that you're not alone, and you have options. You don't have to be bullied all the time."

"Options?" Thea asked.

Danny's cell phone rang, and he held a hand up. "Give me a second." He put the phone to his ear. "Detective Cox."

"Detective Cox, this is dispatch; we have a report of a deceased victim on the pier. Detective Jones to meet you at the scene. Can we text you the address?"

"Please do." Danny's heart was already racing in his chest. "Sweetheart, I'm just saying you can stand up for yourself. You don't have to take the bullying, okay?" He wasn't really paying attention as she agreed. "Okay, love you, honey. I gotta go to work."

Hurrying out of the room, he bumped into Lexie, who saw him rushing and put her hands on her hips. "Did you speak to her?"

"Yes," Danny kissed her, "But then I got a call to go to a scene."

"It's probably not him, Danny," she said gently.

Danny frowned. "I don't always assume it's Jack Waters, but I know he's not gone, babe. I know he's biding his time."

Lexie sighed and held her hands up. "Okay, go to the scene. I'll get the kids to school."

"Love you," he murmured, giving her a quick kiss on the lips before racing downstairs to his safe to get his gun, holster, and badge.

He got into his car and backed out of the driveway. His next-door neighbor tried to flag him down, but he turned a blind eye and raced off, turning on the sirens of his vehicle.

While racing through the neighborhood, he checked his phone for the address, and once he knew where he was going, he pocketed it and focused on the road.

He was at the scene within half an hour and saw that Richard Jones was already there. They had requested they be made partners since they worked so well together on the Bullseye case, and they had been cracking down on criminals together in the year Jack Waters had been missing.

Richard was also the only one who could tolerate Danny's obsession with Bullseye. Danny was constantly getting new 'leads' and 'information' and spending a lot of his downtime chasing them down or poring over the evidence. Richard kept bringing him back to reality.

Richard stood outside the crime scene tape, waiting for his partner to park. As Danny approached, Richard held out a cup of coffee. "Morning, go-go juice?"

"Yeah, thanks." Danny took the cup and slurped a sip. "Still hot, at least."

"I just got here," Richard grinned, "Just waiting for them to finish up processing the scene before I step in. Apparently, there was a lot littered around the body, and they wanted to document and collect it all before allowing us in."

Danny nodded and sipped his coffee again, his eyes moving up the trail to where the crime scene technicians were working around a body propped up on a bench holding a newspaper.

"What have we got so far?" Danny asked.

"Victim is a young male according to witnesses. They pulled his cap off because they thought he was asleep, but it turns out he was shot in the head."

Danny looked at Richard so fast that his neck could have snapped. "In the center of the forehead?"

"No," Richard raised an eyebrow, "Not like Bullseye, Danny. Just a single shot to the head, that's all."

Danny's mind raced, but he tried to listen to what else Richard had to say.

"Witnesses found him around an hour ago and called it in, but one technician reckons he's been here at least most of the night." Richard sighed. "Danny, it's not Bullseye; get your mind away from that case, and focus on the now."

"I know I can't just assume it's Bullseye, but it's partly his MO." Danny frowned. "Single gunshot to the head, and if it's not in the center of the forehead, then he wouldn't have cut the flesh."

"Yeah, he also didn't pose bodies for show," Richard pointed out as the technicians came to them.

"You guys can wear these." The technician handed them plastic booties for their shoes. "And glove up. Leave the coffee behind, and you can start assessing the scene."

They downed their coffees and tossed the cups before putting on the booties and gloves. They carefully crossed under the tape cordoning off the area and walked toward the victim slowly, taking in everything the scene had to offer.

"Won't be possible to get decent footprints. This is a well-used trail to the pier," Richard pointed out.

Danny nodded in agreement.

They approached the body. It was sitting up. There was wire threaded through the bench to its limbs and torso to keep it in place. The newspaper was lying on his lap but seemed glued to his hands. Danny used his pen to lift the front page of the newspaper.

"It's from last year," Danny said, "January last year."

Richard made a note in his book. "Could be relevant. What do you think the motive is?"

"It was clearly done on purpose, too intricate for a hit. Maybe someone out for revenge? Someone a bit insane?" Danny knelt by the body and looked at the bullet wound carefully. "The wound's exit is the front; he was shot from the back."

Richard knelt on the other side of the victim. "I say

let them take the body, and we can try to identify him while they test the wire and glue and other particulars on the body."

"Coroner will identify him faster than we will; let's go with the body." Danny stood up.

"I disagree. Let's not get in their way." Richard stood up as well.

Danny sighed. "Fine, let's go to the station and search missing persons."

Richard smiled. "Why do you even argue with me?"

Danny shook his head, glancing back at the body one last time as he walked away. "Are they canvassing for witnesses?"

"Yeah, but so far, they haven't found any." Richard lifted the tape for Danny to move under it before he followed.

Danny paused until Richard was beside him again. "I'll see you at the station. From there, we can take your car to the coroner." After Richard nodded, Danny went to his car, got in, and started it up.

He pulled into the traffic and drummed his fingers on the steering wheel. His mind raced with the possibilities; he knew that everyone thought he was crazy and obsessed with Bullseye, but a serial killer doesn't just stop killing. And could it be a coincidence that this victim was shot in the head? Possibly, he would admit that. But there was no harm in exploring Bullseye as an option.

He ran through possible scenarios on his drive, and once he reached the station, he struggled to find parking. A message came through on his cell, but before he could look at it, Richard knocked on his window.

"Hurry up," he said loudly.

Danny pocketed his phone and climbed out of his car, locking it behind him. Walking to their desks, Danny put his gun in the top drawer before falling into his chair lazily and turning on his computer screen.

"You check missing persons from the last month," Richard sat down at the desk opposite his, "I'll check older than that."

Danny nodded and set his search parameters, waiting for the slow system to spew back results. He started with the most recent results first, scrolling through each photo, trying to see if any of them looked like their victim. The minutes ticked by, and Danny's mind felt numb from searching through the pictures. The phone on his desk rang, startling him slightly.

"Detective Cox," he answered.

"Doctor Florentine here, Danny," Danny could feel the warm smile the coroner undoubtedly had on his face, "And I have good news. Your victim has been identified."

"That was fast," Danny frowned, picking up a pen, "How did you identify him so quickly?"

"It was luck, actually," Dr. Florentine explained. "One of the medical students at the laboratories knows him. Donovan Ro, a popular trail hiker from the suburbs. I managed to pull up his information on the DMV and have emailed you his details."

"Thanks, Doc." Danny signaled to Richard. "Tell the student they better be right, or I'm coming for them."

"I assure you, I checked, and the fingerprints matched. It's Mr. Ro."

Dr. Florentine hung up the phone, and Danny stood, leaning over his keyboard and using his mouse to check his emails. The email from the coroner's office popped up, and he quickly printed out the information he needed.

"He's been identified?" Richard stood up, putting his jacket back on.

"Some kid recognized him," Danny explained. "He's into hiking. Florentine pulled his information up on the DMV and got a hit."

"We going to break the news to the family?"

Danny grabbed the paper from the printer and looked at the information. "Says he's married, so best we do that."

Once on their way, with Richard driving, Danny mused out loud, "The real question is, what is the motive? Apparently, this guy likes to hike. Sounds like an ordinary Joe to me."

"You never know with some people," Richard reminded him. "People put on an act, and then they turn out to be real freaks."

Danny shrugged; he knew Richard wasn't wrong, but he let his mind wander as they drove, keeping his thoughts about Bullseye to himself.

They drove into a nice quiet suburb, and the navigation system took them right up to a beautiful, all-American house. White picket fence, dog playing outside, two kids running around the yard. The only thing that was off was the patrol car parked outside. The detectives looked at each other once the car was in park and then climbed out.

The two kids stopped playing to watch as they walked up the path to the front door. Danny waved, but they didn't wave back. Richard knocked on the door, and a voice called, "Don?" before swinging the door open rather violently.

A bereft-looking woman with puffy eyes stood in front of them. Her shoulders sank as she saw the two men in suits standing outside. "I'm sorry, I don't know what you're selling, but I don't have time for it now."

"We're detectives, ma'am," Richard showed his badge, and Danny followed, "We're here to speak to you about your husband."

"They've already sent a patrol car out to take down his details for the missing person's case," she sniffed, tears threatening to spill again, "I'm sorry they sent you as well."

"Ma'am, it's not that." Danny was as gentle as he could be. "Can we come inside to speak to you?"

She looked fearful and stepped aside. She led them to where two police officers were sitting in the living room.

"Officers." Richard nodded, recognizing them.

"Detectives, are you here to take over?" the one uniform asked.

"Yes, you can go, thank you." Danny waved them off. The two detectives sat opposite Mrs. Ro, and after a moment, it was Danny who spoke.

"Mrs. Ro, your husband's body was found this morning at the pier," he said quietly. "It appears as though he was murdered."

She stared at them for the longest time, and yet it felt like no time passed at all when she was suddenly wailing. They sat in front of her awkwardly as she sobbed loudly into her hands; her young son and daughter came racing inside the house to see what was wrong.

"Mommy, what's wrong? Mommy," they pleaded with her, touching her gently, showing her so much compassion for children their age.

Sam pulled her children to her and held them tightly for a long time before shaking her head. "I'll explain it to you later," her voice was raw with emotion, "Go outside and have fun."

"Are you sure?" Ollie asked.

"Go," Sam said, and they left. She took a few deep breaths and tried to compose herself.

"Do you know who did it?" It was a plea.

"Not yet," Richard explained. "Did your husband have any enemies? Any secrets he may have kept from you?"

"No," Sam glared at them, "Don't try and make out like this is my husband's fault. He was a good man; we just celebrated his birthday."

"Was that the day he went missing?" Danny flipped open his notebook to take notes.

"Yes," Sam looked out the window, "He liked to hike to clear his mind; we gave him new gear. He said he'd be back in an hour, and we haven't seen him since. How do I explain to my kids that their father was murdered?" She looked at them with wide eyes.

"I would suggest involving a family counselor, ma'am," Danny said gently. "Especially if you're unsure."

Sam shook her head. "This isn't happening. This can't be happening. Why would someone want to murder my husband?"

Richard glanced at Danny and then leaned on his knees with his elbows. "Mrs. Ro, the way he was...he was posed at the crime scene, makes us suspect that it was either very personal or there's a significant reason he was chosen."

"Chosen?" Sam asked. "Like a cult chose him?"

Danny shook his head. "We don't want to jump to conclusions. It could be a nut job who he met somewhere who took advantage of a situation; we won't know until we have the full reports back from our teams."

"Then what are you doing here? You've told me he's dead; go find his killer." There it was, the anger. Danny and Richard were used to it.

"If you think of anything, and I mean anything, no matter how small, that you think would be helpful, please reach me on this number," Richard explained as he took out and handed her a business card.

They climbed back into Richard's vehicle. "The coroner?" Danny asked.

"I think so." Richard nodded, starting the car and pulling into the road.

"He does look like he was an average Joe; maybe it is just some lunatic," Danny mused. "Or..."

"Here we go," Richard sighed. "How is it connected to Bullseye?"

Danny looked at him. "Don't get me wrong, it's a different MO, but maybe Waters is changing his MO to screw with us, so we don't think he is linked to this."

"Danny, until we find concrete evidence that this is Jack Waters, we are not telling anyone your Bullseye theory," Richard said sternly. "You'll possibly set off a wild goose chase, and I'll look like an idiot too for indulging you."

Danny frowned and looked out the window. "Fine, but just know I'm working it in the background."

"Fine."

They didn't speak for the rest of the journey.

They entered the coroner's office and stopped at the front desk. "Hi, June," Richard said with a flirtatious smile, "Is Florentine in?"

"He's busy with your victim now," she looked over her horn-rimmed glasses at him, "Off you go, don't waste my time." The elderly receptionist had always been no-nonsense.

"Aw, you break my heart, June," Richard teased before Danny chuckled and pushed him down the hallway.

"Come on, lover boy."

They walked to the morgue and peeked in, seeing Florentine with Donovan's corpse exposed on the gurney.

"Anything interesting?" Richard asked as they walked in.

"Lots, actually," the doctor said without looking up. "For one thing, I can confirm it was the gunshot to the head that killed him, but then it gets really interesting."

They put on gloves and masks and approached the body.

"He was opened up post mortem," Florentine explained, "I found evidence of someone with surgical skills to have opened him up. They also removed his heart and replaced it with this."

Florentine turned and lifted a bag that contained a cube. He passed it to Danny, who held it up.

"It says something on the cube," he murmured.

"It says January," the doctor said with a somber voice. "I think this could be the start of someone's dance with death."

"A serial killer? We need more than one body to declare that," Richard took the cube and looked at it, "What's inside the cube?"

"I'm saying if January is anything to go by, February comes next." Dr. Florentine held his hand out for the bag. "We're going to test what kind of gem is in the cube and let you know. Maybe you can trace where this came from."

Danny and Richard looked down at Donovan, and then Richard pointed to his ankle. "Was that broken before or after death?"

"Before; from the scrapes and bruises, it looks like he fell from a great height, down a hill or cliff perhaps. I found plant debris and soil in the cuts. I would suggest investigating the trails he liked to hike." Dr. Florentine leaned over the body again. "That's all I have for now; you'll have my report when I'm done. No point in hovering."

The two detectives disposed of their gloves and masks and left.

"It could take us weeks to figure out which trail he was on," Danny said with a sigh.

"Best we get cracking then." Richard led him out of the building.

They were outside on the steps when Danny's phone rang, and he pulled it out of his pocket. "It's my wife," he told Richard before answering, "Hi, honey."

Richard watched as Danny's face contorted and then changed to a look of shock.

"Yeah, I'll come down to the school. I'll meet you there," Danny said before hanging up.

"Everything okay?" Richard asked.

"Can I drop you at the station? I have to go to the school; my daughter is in the principal's office. They might suspend her." Danny ran a hand over his face and sighed.

"Sure, no problem, Danny. I'm sure it's just a misunderstanding," Richard assured him as they climbed into the car. "Was it Cleo?"

"Thea," Danny sighed, "She never gets into trouble."

"It's probably just a misunderstanding," Richard said again.

Danny stopped at the station to drop Richard off. Richard agreed to look up some places they could visit while Danny sorted Thea out.

Luckily there wasn't much traffic to test Danny's temper as he drove to the school. He found a parking spot and climbed out, seeing Lexie's car parked a few spots away. It had been Lexie who had called him, just as surprised as he was that they were being summoned to the school.

Lexie was waiting outside of the principal's office with Thea, another girl, and two adults that were livid. It had to be the girl's parents. The blonde-haired cheerleader's eye was swollen shut.

"Great, we're all here." Principal Greggory clapped his hands; Danny hadn't seen him hanging around just behind Lexie. "Please come in and take a seat."

They all filed in. Danny and the other father let the mothers take the seats while the girls stood awkwardly to the side.

"Now, I'm sure you're all aware of why we're here," Principal Greggory said, but Lexie put up her hand.

"No, we don't. We were just told to come in."

"Your daughter attacked ours for no reason," the mother spat at Lexie. "I want her suspended."

"Whoa, whoa, whoa!" Danny frowned. "Thea would never hurt a fly, and even if she did do that, what did your daughter do to deserve it?"

"How dare you?" the girl's father said. "You'll be lucky if I don't sue you! I'll open a case against your child for assault."

Principal Greggory held up his hands. "Now, now, we cannot prove who started the fight."

"She did," Thea said suddenly. "She's always bullying me. I've been to the guidance counselor lots of times about it. My dad said that I could handle it and stand up for myself."

All the adults looked at Danny, who paled slightly. "I didn't mean resort to physical violence, honey. I meant that you could call them out for it. Report it."

"I'm sure Thea is really sorry for what she's done," Lexie started to say, but Thea cut her off.

"No, I'm not. She tortures me every day."

"Just look how she speaks to adults," the other mother pointed to Thea, "And you don't think she started this? Clearly, the problem starts at home."

"Hey!" Lexie and Danny both raised their voices. Soon all the adults were insulting each other, and Principal Greggory tried to restore calm. Once everyone was quiet again, he sighed.

"Thea got physical, so she's suspended for a week."

Danny stepped forward. "What does the bully get?"

Greggory raised his hands before the adults could start fighting again. "She didn't get physical, so she is not suspended, but she will have detention for two Saturdays for bullying."

The adults were in an uproar again. The Cox's because of the unfair punishment and the other parents because they felt their daughter did nothing wrong, as the school had no proof.

Greggory shook his head and raised his voice, "It's done. It's final. Thea will be sent her work, so she doesn't fall behind."

The other family left in a huff, and Danny followed with Lexie and Thea following him. They stopped outside at Lexie's car, and Lexie opened her car door. "Get in," she snapped. "You are grounded."

"But Dad said I could," Thea whined, tears forming in her eyes.

Lexie shook her head. "No arguments."

As soon as Thea was in the car, Danny ran a hand over his face. "Lexie, I didn't say she could beat—"

"You were distracted, weren't you?" Lexie turned to face him with anger in her eyes. "What happened? Hm? Think of a lead? Get a call?"

"Lexie, you know my work—"

"Is more important than your family, I get it," her words dripped with venom, and Danny glared at her.

"That's not it at all; I told Thea she could stand up for herself."

"Well, now she's got a mark on her school record, which is going to look great for college applications, Danny. But tell me what it was?" Lexie crossed her arms.

Danny sighed and held up his hands. "I got a call. But I didn't—"

"Of course, you did," Lexie fumed. "Why don't you go back to your precious Bullseye, and I'll sort our daughter out like I always have to do on my own."

She spun around without another word, ignoring Danny's protests, and climbed into the driver's side.

Danny stepped out of the way as she pulled out and drove off. He walked to his car and kicked his tire. "Dammit!"

He climbed into his car and pulled out his phone, dialing Richard's number. "Tell me you have something?"

"Doctor Florentine says the stone is a garnet stone, which is readily available, but I searched it in connection with the word January, and it turns out it's one of the January birthstones," Richard rattled off.

"Have we got anywhere we can go look?" Danny asked, exasperated.

Richard paused and then said, "Well, I was going to check out a store that might sell these cube things. It's a holistic store."

"What makes you think we should try there?" Danny asked.

"I don't know, January birthstones sound like something those astrological-loving folk would be into," Richard commented. "Are you going to meet me there?"

"Text me the address." Danny hung up and waited for the message.

Once it came through, he punched it into his GPS and pulled out, trying to put his family woes out of his mind. The more he tried to focus on work, though, the more his thoughts trailed back to what Lexie had said.

He knew it had always been hard for her to have a

husband with a dangerous and demanding job; he had missed a lot over the years, and Lexie had always forgiven him. It was just them, after all, both sets of their parents were buried, and they had no siblings. He would find a way to make it up to her.

He pulled up to the store and saw Richard standing there with his hands on his hips.

"It's closed," Richard announced as Danny approached. "Suppose we should try again some other time, but for now," he handed Danny a long list on a piece of paper, "jewelry stores; you check those, and I'll check my list, and let's see if anyone ever sold these cube things."

"Okay, but it feels like a waste of time." Danny sighed. "We should be looking for the trail the guy was on."

"I have some patrol officers checking out the local places; hopefully, they'll come back with something." Richard looked at him and asked, "Are you okay? Did everything go okay?"

"Lexie's pissed because I told my daughter to stand up for herself, then got distracted by work. Thea took that to mean to physically stand up for herself, and now she's suspended." Danny's shoulders sank. "She's seriously pissed. Think I'll be on the couch tonight."

Richard clapped a hand on his shoulder. "It's okay, Danny, it's just the pressures of being a teenager's parent, I'm sure. Things will get better, just take her some flowers or get her something at one of these jewelry stores."

"Like I can afford that," Danny scoffed, "But flowers...maybe. I'll also try to get home early. Right, let's do this; I'll call in later to check up on you."

They parted ways.

CHAPTER 3

2014 - 15 Years Old

They had been camping for two weeks, living off the land deep within the forest they lived in, with not another human being anywhere near them. This section of the forest was strictly off-limits, but no one knew they were there or that they lived there. The forest was huge, and it was easy to hide in.

Father had wanted to teach Hunter about trapping larger animals. They had spent most of their time digging pits and setting traps to try and catch wild pigs, but they hadn't managed to get anything yet. Hunter was impatient; he wanted to track and shoot a wild pig and be done with this exercise, but he didn't dare say anything to Father.

On the first day of the third week, he heard Father stirring before dawn. He got dressed quickly and exited his tent, finding Father by the fire with his rifle. Hunter sat on a log near the fire and waited quietly.

"Today, we drive them to the traps; they are dangerous animals, so make sure you drive them away and don't attract them to charge you. You need to be the alpha in this situation."

Hunter nodded, listening in respectful silence. Father passed him a plate of roasted rabbit meat, something from their earlier kills. Hunter ate in silence, and once done, they rinsed off their dishes and packed up their campsite to prevent predators from getting in.

Hunter grabbed his rifle and carefully followed Father into the forest, past the places where they had set traps. The forest was waking up around them as the sun slowly crested the skyline; however, it still remained dark within the trees.

Father held his fist up to indicate Hunter was to stop.

"Go downwind and drive them. I'll go upwind and do the same. Go about half a click; they'll be in a clearing up ahead."

Hunter didn't know how Father knew that, but he immediately took off to the left, making as little noise as possible as he walked.

He listened for the giveaway grunts of the wild pigs

that he needed to find. It was half an hour before he heard them.

He crouched down and slowly approached the clearing where they were feeding. It was a small sounder of them. Hunter's eyes landed on the large male toward the back. If he could bring that back to Father, he was sure he would be pleased.

Hunter aimed his rifle and fired a shot near the large beast, and although it was startled, it didn't run away in the opposite direction. The rest of the sounder took off into the trees, but the male snorted and ground its hoof into the forest floor before seeing Hunter as he slowly stood, rifle still raised.

He let off another shot to scare the animal, but instead of fleeing, it charged him. Hunter turned and ran as quickly as he could.

The wild animal made loud noises as he pursued him, and Hunter had to let go of his gun to run faster as it was inhibiting him. He tossed it into the brush and continued to run, picking up his pace. Hunter tried to gather his bearings as he moved, but he was practically flying through the woods.

He recognized a clearing near the river and turned right sharply. He knew there was a trap nearby; he just had to find it and lure the animal in there. He could see where the ground was disturbed and sprinted straight toward it, knowing the pig was on his heels. As he reached the edge of the trap, he leaped over it, landing hard with a loud crunching sound as his ankle broke.

The pig stopped at the edge of the pit, despite it being covered, and stomped its hooves. It snuffled the ground, and then to Hunter's horror, it made its way around the trap instead of into it. Hunter tried to crawl away, trying not to cry out in pain.

The animal was approaching closer each moment, and Hunter was on his ass, trying to use his good leg to push himself backward, his hands getting cut up by the stones and sticks on the forest floor.

The pig squealed as a shot rang out, the pig keeling over, panting.

Father exited the forest to the side of Hunter, his face as cold as marble. He walked up to the pig and shot it in the head before turning to look at Hunter.

"Unacceptable," his voice was dripping in disappointment. Now out of danger, Hunter found a stick strong enough to hold his weight and struggled to his feet, leaning on the stick like a crutch.

Father used some rope to tie the pig's feet together and dragged it off through the forest without a backward glance to see if Hunter was following.

They reached their campsite, and Father lifted the pig onto the back of their truck.

"Pack up your things."

Hunter went as quickly as he could, but the pain in

his ankle was unbearable. He packed everything badly and tossed it in the back of the truck defiantly. Father climbed into the driver's side without helping Hunter into the passenger side.

They sat in silence as they made their way back to their cabin. The trip took almost two hours, driving slowly through the forest. Once they saw the bushes that marked the start of their territory, Father finally spoke.

"Strip and hang."

Hunter looked at him wide-eyed.

"You know what you've done is unacceptable. You lost your weapon, and you lost control of the situation. You acted foolishly. I'm going to give you a reminder that will stick with you for life so you won't do it again."

Hunter swallowed and nodded, knowing better than to argue.

Father stopped the truck, and using his stick, Hunter made his way into the shed instead of the cabin itself. He pulled a small set of steps to the post in the middle of the shed, and with great difficulty, he climbed them. He slipped his hands through two leather strands that were looped at the top of the beam.

Father came in after him, his leather belt in his hand, wrapped once around, and he moved the steps out of the way, so Hunter was dangling, his muscles bulging from holding his weight.

Father calmly watched him for a moment before saying, "Don't ever lose your weapon."

He struck Hunter three times, and the boy grit his teeth before repeating, "I must never lose my weapon."

Father was completely calm. "I will not be arrogant when I hunt, no matter what I'm hunting."

Three strikes, and Hunter grunted out the same words.

This went on for several lashes before Father brought the steps back to Hunter and put his belt back on.

"Go upstairs and wrap that ankle; you can rest tomorrow, but then I want you back to your chores. I don't care how you get them done. The world isn't fair and won't wait for you to heal. It continues to move regardless of what happens."

Hunter nodded, trying his best to bite back the tears that threatened to spill.

He hobbled out of the shed and toward the cabin, glancing at the pig on the back of the truck. Father slapped him on the back of the head.

"If you don't want me to make you skin this kill, then hurry your ass up."

Hunter went as quickly as he could, making his way upstairs to his room, where he kept a first aid kit.

Only when he was alone did he allow himself to cry. He had to make it quick and hide it because if Father saw it, he would be taught his lessons again.

There was no room for emotions in their lives. They were chosen with purpose, and their purpose had to come first, before their own feelings and pain. Hunter knew this; he knew Father was only doing what was right. He would be fine.

The world continued to turn regardless of who was hurt or died; it stopped for nothing. Not until the day it would be destroyed.

2021 - PRESENT DAY

February - Bianca

Bianca couldn't remember the last time she had been on a blind date, but she was excited. She had been talking to Wayne for a few weeks now, and he seemed like an amazing guy.

The best part was he had planned a secret surprise for her birthday. She couldn't wait to see what he had up his sleeve. They had agreed they were dating around the third week they had been chatting. Many people thought Bianca was insane, but she just felt such a connection with him.

She had specifically booked a nail and hair appointment at her favorite salon for this. When she arrived, the owner, Julia, smiled brightly.

"What are we doing today then?" she asked.

Bianca gave her a wide-toothed grin. "I want the

usual for my hair, but something ombre for my nails, like a blue that matches my eyes fading to white."

"Sounds fantastic. Let's get you going." Julia led her to the basin.

They would do her nails while Julia did the highlights in her hair. They were really efficient, which was one of the reasons that Bianca loved them so much.

When they were done, they swiveled her chair around so she could look at herself in the mirror. Her brown hair with streaks of blonde looked fantastic, and her nails were done exactly as she imagined. She squealed.

"You are all amazing," she declared, standing up and picking up her purse. She took out two tens and tipped the nail ladies before going to the counter to pay and tip Julia.

"Thanks so much, Bianca, and happy birthday, by the way," she smiled. "We got you a little something as our favorite customer."

"Aw, you guys didn't have to do that," Bianca gushed as Julia produced a gift bag.

Bianca smiled brightly and pulled out the beautiful blue dress in her size. "Oh, guys, it's perfect. I love you guys so much!"

She went around and hugged each of them, lingering by Julia a little longer.

Julia patted her back and grinned. "Enjoy your date tonight. I want to hear all about it."

"I can't believe I'm finally going to meet him," Bianca giggled. "I'm so excited, and I'm so wearing this dress tonight."

Bianca said her goodbyes and left the salon in high spirits. She went to her Mini Cooper parked a short way away and climbed in, setting the gift bag on the passenger seat.

She checked her phone, but there were no new messages. Wayne had said he would let her know the plans when the time was right, and it was exciting and nerve-wracking all at the same time.

She pulled into the driveway of her large condo and parked, climbing out with her gift bag and heading inside. She loved the condo that her parents had bought for her; it even came with a glass swimming pool that had a great view.

Everything was open and spacious and clean, especially since her dad paid a maid to come in every day. Bianca would admit she was a tad bit spoiled. She didn't have to work yet, but that was the benefit of having a well-off family, and she saw nothing wrong with that.

She made herself a healthy snack, and while she ate it in her sun nook, her phone went off. It was Wayne, telling her that he was taking her on a romantic walk and picnic.

She excitedly replied that she couldn't wait to see him, and he responded, confirming he felt the same. He sent her the address and told her to meet him there at six, just before the sun went down, so they could watch the sunset.

Bianca wondered if wearing the blue dress was a good idea if they were going for a walk. She supposed she could pair it with some cute white tennis shoes for comfort.

She went to get ready, and it took her no time before she was standing in front of the mirror examining herself. She looked perfect, with just a light touch of makeup, and her outfit looked super cute.

Confident, she checked her phone for the address, and seeing that Wayne sent it, she checked the time. She calculated how long it would take her to get there and decided to leave straight away in case there was traffic.

As she drove, she put on some music quite loudly and jammed to it, bouncing in her seat and singing her heart out.

She was taking singing lessons too because she really believed she had a shot at becoming a popular artist; everyone she met loved her singing, so music was a big part of her life.

There was traffic, but she didn't mind; she just continued to rock out to the various songs on her thumb drive that was plugged into her car. Some people looked at her as though she was crazy, but many people simply smiled or laughed at her, and she smiled back.

She pulled into the parking lot of the south entrance

to the national forest outside the city. She climbed out of her car and made sure it was locked, pulling her purse onto her shoulder. She checked herself in the reflection of the driver's side window before taking out her phone and texting Wayne.

It took him five minutes to respond, but he did, telling her to walk toward the hiking trails and, instead of taking them, veer off right and follow the small footpath; she'd find their picnic there.

Excited and nervous, Bianca tried not to walk too fast; she didn't want to break into a sweat before their first date. It wasn't hard to find the footpath, and while the sun slowly set, she started to make her way along it.

A bit nervous, she took out her phone and used it as a flashlight. The forest buzzed around her, and she worried some wild animal might attack her.

Up ahead, she saw a blanket spread out in a clearing and immediately relaxed. She had made it. She turned, kept her phone's light trained on the path ahead of her, and concentrated, looking down, not wanting to trip over anything until she reached Wayne.

She had just reached the end of the path and looked up when the gunshot rang out and went straight through her right eye. She sunk to the floor.

Dead.

Hunter didn't flinch as he walked forward and started to pack up the picnic things. After he was done, he retrieved Bianca's body and loaded it into the back of his truck before climbing in and driving back toward the cabin they called home.

Father was sitting at the kitchen table when he walked in with Bianca's body draped over his shoulder. He carried her downstairs, and Father got up and followed.

Hunter stood to the side and allowed Father to examine her. He wasn't sure what Father was looking for, but after he was done, he nodded. "You can proceed."

Father ascended the stairs, and Hunter immediately got to work, getting the blue dress off of Bianca and then her underwear.

He cracked up her chest as he had with Donovan and removed her heart, placing it in a jar. He then retrieved the second glass cube from the wooden box and inspected it before placing it in her chest and starting to close her up.

He stitched her carefully before dressing her in a red dress and heels. He checked her makeup wasn't smudged and gathered her body in his arms, taking her back upstairs. It was pitch dark outside as he loaded her into the back and covered her with a tarp.

He went back inside and showered, changing his clothes and pulling a cap over his face before grabbing a bag and heading for the door.

Father didn't look up as he said, "Don't get caught or seen."

Hunter paused and replied, "Yes, Father."

He walked out and to the driver's side of his truck, climbed in, and started to drive for the forest, intending to head for the city.

CHAPTER 4

HIGH STREET, MIDTOWN

Danny woke up holding onto Lexie. He stroked her side gently before kissing her bare shoulder and getting up. He wanted to get in early today to work on a few cases he needed to catch up on, and he didn't want to wake Lexie or the girls when he left. He got dressed in the bathroom after washing up and brushing his teeth. He pulled his shoes on, and as he was leaving when Lexie stirred.

"Danny," she murmured.

Danny knelt by her side of the bed. "I'm going now, babe. I'll see you tonight." He leaned forward and kissed her lips softly.

She murmured something in her sleep but didn't stir again, so Danny left. Downstairs he made himself a cup of coffee in his traveling mug, holstered his gun, and put on his badge before walking out of the house.

The neighborhood was silent as he backed out of his drive, a lone jogger making their way down the street with their Labrador. Nothing else stirred. Danny loved this time of day.

He pulled onto the main road where traffic was just starting and drove toward the station. He hummed softly as he drove, not thinking about anything in particular.

A teenager suddenly cycled out in front of his car, and he slammed on the brakes. The kid tipped over, and Danny put his emergency signals on before climbing out of the car. He approached the kid.

"Hey, are you okay?" He helped the mousy-haired boy to his feet.

"Yes, sorry, sir, I was in a rush because I'm late for my paper route."

"Well, look both ways, 'cause no paper route is worth your life, kid," Danny said. "You're not hurt, right?"

He shook his head and climbed back on his bike. "Thanks for stopping, mister. Most people just yell."

"No problem, kid, get out of here." Danny climbed back into his car and turned off his emergency signals before pulling off again. He took a deep breath and then reached for his coffee, sipping it slowly.

He pulled into the parking lot of the station and

found a spot close to the entrance. He locked his car and took his coffee into the building.

The building was always busy, twenty-four hours a day, seven days a week. He greeted people as he passed them, and finally, he made it to his desk.

He started to work on his case files immediately. He made notes of follow-up calls he had to make, got up to make copies of the files he needed to drop at court, and typed up reports that were due.

He was so caught up with his work that he was genuinely surprised when Richard set a cup of coffee on his desk. "Good morning. What time did you get here?'

"Just after half five." Danny took the cup and sipped it, smacking his lips. "Didn't realize I'd been here long. What's it now, seven?"

"Eight," Richard replied, chuckling. "I don't come in early, remember?"

"I can hope," Danny teased, setting his coffee down. He leaned back in his chair. "How was the night out?"

Richard sat in his chair and shrugged. "We had dinner, I wined and dined her, and we went back to her place where things got interesting."

"Did you leave your number this morning? Or take hers?"

Richard smiled mischievously. "You know I never call, and I tell them all that when I ask them out. If they hope to change me, that's on them."

Danny shook his head. "One day, someone is going to hook you, Richard, and you'll be better for it."

Richard simply chuckled and turned to his own files.

They weren't working for more than forty-five minutes when their new captain approached their tables. "Boys, I got a fresh one for you; think you may have seen something like this before." He held up a piece of paper with an address. "Shot to the head, and the body was posed."

Richard shot Danny a warning look and said, "Sounds like the Ro case; was this at the pier again?"

"High Street, Midtown," Captain Baker explained. "But thought you'd like it."

Danny reached for the paper he held up. "Yeah, we'll go check it out right now."

The captain left, and they got up from their desks, taking their guns out of their desk drawers and holstering them.

"We'll take my car." Richard grabbed his keys and led the way out.

They hadn't even pulled out of the parking garage before Richard started on Danny, "It's not Bullseye, Danny. There are other sick serial killers out there, *if* this is the same guy."

Danny rolled his eyes. "Rich, seriously, I get it. You don't have to harp on at me about it."

"Except I do because that's what you focus on."

"Don't you have a case that's haunted you?" Danny

asked. "One that was left undone and that you want to make sure is closed before your time is done?"

"Danny, we'll find him; I'm just saying don't let your obsession with him cloud your judgment of this case." Richard sighed. "Please."

"I'll take that as a no." Danny looked out his window, and they fell silent.

They saw the cordoned-off area as they turned the corner onto High Street. Richard parked on the pavement, and they climbed out of his car, heading toward the bright tape that marked the start of the crime scene. They flashed their badges and were asked to wait for a crime scene technician to clear them.

They only waited a few minutes before they were handed gloves and plastic booties to put on. They then ducked under the tape and made their way toward a small outdoor dining area.

It was surrounded by wrought iron fencing that came to Danny's hip. Easy to climb over. Most of the chairs were turned upside down on the tables except one where a woman was sitting upright, her lifeless eyes staring ahead. There was wire wrapped around strategic parts of her body to keep her in place. She had a newspaper folded on her lap.

Danny hovered in front of her, inspecting her closely while Richard knelt to get a different perspective.

"Must be between twenty and twenty-five," Richard

guessed. "It looks like she's out on a date, the way she's dressed."

"Think she knew the killer?" Danny wondered.

Richard shook his head. "I honestly don't know; it would be nice if she did because then we can have a decent suspect pool."

Danny turned to the crime scene technician. "Any purse? Form of identification?"

The young woman whose tag read Kim shook her head. "No, nothing to identify her."

Danny sighed and ran a hand over his balding head. "Shit."

"Looks like she just got her hair and nails done," Richard commented.

Danny frowned. "How can you tell?"

Richard raised an eyebrow. "I dated a beautician a couple of times back in the day; you learn a thing or two."

Danny nodded. "Okay, so she must have gone to a salon sometime recently. There's only like a thousand legal salons in the city, never mind the illegal ones, so that's narrowed it down."

"My, my, my," Richard shook his head, "Chill out, Danny, you're losing your cool."

Danny glared at him, and then his glare softened into an apologetic look. "Just feeling frustrated, a lot of unsolved cases at the moment."

Richard nodded his understanding and glanced

around. "There's a crowd forming; we better let them take the body."

They walked toward the tape where people were gathering.

"We need to identify her as soon as possible," Danny commented as they ducked under the tape.

As they walked away, an older lady came up to them. "Excuse me, Detectives, I couldn't help but overhear you. I think I can help."

Richard and Danny shared a look before Danny asked, "And how is that?"

"I can't be positive, but I'm sure that's Howard Pike's daughter," she dabbed at her eyes, "He's a prominent businessman, owns a firm uptown. His wife is in my social circle."

Richard frowned. "Are you having us on, ma'am? Cause it's a high coincidence that you would know the victim."

"Wait, I think I have a photo of her, and please call me Shirl."

The detectives waited as Shirl battled shakily with her smartphone, scrolling through dozens of pictures. Danny was going to excuse them when she suddenly smiled. "Aha, here is a nice one of her."

She turned the phone to the detectives, and they inspected it. Danny frowned. "Can I borrow your phone quickly?"

"Yes, but please don't delete my photos; some are of my grandchildren."

"I just want to compare the photo to the body," Danny assured her.

He and Richard went back to the body, which was now on a gurney, and Danny held the photo up. "Well, I'll be damned. It is her."

Richard hurried back to Shirl. "What is Mr. Pike's daughter's name?"

"Beatrice? Betty? No, that's not it," Shirl looked worried, "Bianca! It's Bianca! Lovely girl, though a bit spoiled."

Danny came back and returned her phone. "I've sent the photo to myself," he told her. "Thank you for your help, ma'am. Can you please give your contact information to the patrolman here?" He indicated an officer nearby. "And we'll contact you if we have any other questions."

Shirl nodded, and Danny and Richard ducked down and headed to the car. Richard pulled up his phone and started to tinker on it.

"Howard Pike of Pike, Messi, Charles, and Jones. Big wig," Richard commented. "Mostly represents major corporations, must be well off."

"Let's meet the body at the morgue and ask Florentine to see if Bianca comes up in the DMV or anything so we can confirm and go see Mr. Pike," Danny suggested.

Richard climbed into the driver's side with a quick

nod. They waited for the coroner's van to take off, and they followed it straight to the morgue.

When they walked in, Dr. Florentine looked up. "You're joking, right? They haven't even finished processing the paperwork for your victim yet."

"We have a possible identification; we just need you to confirm it, and we'll leave you to it." Richard held his hands up.

Florentine glared at him and shook his head, picking up something they couldn't see and leaving. They hovered in the room, wondering if they were supposed to follow him when he came back with what looked like a handprint on a piece of card. He put it in a scanner and started clicking away on a computer.

"Possible name?" he snapped.

Danny glanced at Richard. "Bianca Pike."

Dr. Florentine typed on the computer and stood up straight. "It'll take a moment."

"We're really sorry to be a pain," Richard tried to smooth things over.

Florentine rolled his eyes. "Until next time, every cop says that. Every victim is urgent. It's not like I haven't got a ton of bodies to process as it is."

Richard fell silent as a little bell sounded behind Florentine, who checked the screen. "It's a match; your victim is Bianca Pike."

Danny nodded. "Thanks, Doc, and sorry again."

They hurried out of the morgue, and Richard pulled

his phone out. "I've got the address for the firm; her father is probably at work at this time. Probably the best place to catch him."

Danny climbed into the passenger side. "He's going to shit himself. The richest ones always do."

Richard smiled. "Good thing it doesn't get to us then, right?"

Danny snorted as Richard drove them through the city.

They pulled up to a very modern-looking building, and Richard turned into the parking garage that connected it. He was stopped by a guard at the machine that issued parking tickets.

"This parking is for people visiting the law firm only," he explained.

Richard grinned. "That's perfect then because that's exactly where we're headed."

The guard grabbed Richard's hand as he reached out again. "I'm not an idiot, buddy. Get out of here."

Danny rolled his eyes and showed the guard his badge. "We're here for Mr. Pike, so move out of the way, or I'll arrest you for interfering in a murder investigation."

Richard grinned at the guard again as he stammered an apology. After Richard grabbed the ticket, he found parking, and they followed the signs to the law firm's offices. They checked with the front desk which was the correct floor before climbing on the elevator and standing quietly.

"You scared that guy," Richard pointed out.

Danny didn't look at him. "He was arrogant."

Richard murmured an agreement as the elevator chimed, and they stepped off on the top floor. A receptionist was directly in front of them, and Danny approached her, badge out. "Good day, I'm Detective Cox, this is Detective Jones. We need to speak to Mr. Pike."

"I'm sorry, sir, Mr. Pike is not seeing anyone at the moment," the receptionist explained. "You will need to make an appointment to see him, the earliest of which is next week."

Danny stepped out of Richard's way, who threw a flirty smile at the receptionist. "Listen, it's about his daughter. So unless you want him to find out some really bad news from someone else or from us later at his home, and he's going to be pissed at you for not letting us in, then I understand. But I would let us in."

The receptionist's eyes widened, and she picked up the phone. "Yes, sir, I know you didn't want to be disturbed, but there seems to be an emergency, and two detectives need to see you." She listened, hung up, and stood up. "Follow me."

They fell into step behind her and walked down a long corridor to a large open plan office where an older gentleman was sitting going through some papers.

"Gentlemen, I'm a very busy man; can we make this quick?" he said without looking up.

"Sir, it's about your daughter," Danny started to say.

"How much is the bail? Or is it a fine? I'll write a check." He still hadn't looked at them.

Richard put a hand on Danny's arm and stepped forward. "Mr. Pike, your daughter's body was found this morning in Midtown."

Mr. Pike looked up. "Her body?" he asked with a frown. "You must be mistaken. My daughter doesn't hang around with the kind of people that would get her killed. You've got the wrong person."

"Sir, we've done identification by fingerprint," Danny explained. "It confirmed the body was Bianca Pike. This young lady." Danny took out his phone and showed him the picture from Shirl.

Mr. Pike paled. "Who did it? Have you got a suspect? How was she killed?"

Richard shook his head. "We don't have all the details yet, Mr. Pike; the coroner is busy with her body now. She was found in Midtown, and it appears as though she was killed by a gunshot to the head. I'm really sorry for your loss."

Mr. Pike stood up and clasped his hands behind his back, standing by the window looking out in silence. The detectives waited until he spoke again.

"What resources do you need to find her killer? I'll

provide you with everything you need." He turned to look at them. "Name your price."

Danny held up his hands. "We don't need your money, sir. What we need is information, as much information as you can give us."

Mr. Pike sat back down. "What do you need to know? Bianca was a good child, honor roll, was dreaming of being a singer. She lived in a condo not far from Midtown; I can give you keys to the condo if you need to search there. You have my permission."

Danny nodded. "We would appreciate that, sir."

Mr. Pike pushed a button on his telephone. "Jenny, get me Bianca's spare key and write down the details the detectives will need to get to and into her house." He sat back and stared at Danny. "I want this solved."

Danny nodded. "We are going to do our best."

"Not your best, you're going to do it, period," Mr. Pike said dismissively. "I have to go home and inform my wife. Who can we contact about my daughter's body?"

"Someone from the coroner's office will be in touch," Richard explained. "They first have to process her body for clues."

"You can go," Mr. Pike said, waving a hand.

"One quick question," Richard said. "She recently visited a salon. Do you know which one?"

Mr. Pike shook his head. "I don't exactly track...I didn't track Bianca's every move; she was an adult."

"Juls Styles," Jenny said from behind them. "I know because once, for my birthday, she took me there as a gift."

Richard turned to Jenny. "Can you give me those details as well?"

Jenny nodded and left, and Danny turned to Mr. Pike. "Here's my card," he said as he held one out. "Contact me if you can think of anything that might help."

Mr. Pike took the card and set it on his table, swinging his chair around to look out the window.

Richard glanced at Danny before they went down the corridor to Jenny, who gave them the information they needed.

"Let's go to the morgue, then back to the station, then I'll go to the salon, and you can go to her house," Danny suggested.

"Yeah, sounds good." Richard climbed into his car and started it.

Once they were parked outside the morgue, they walked inside, waving at the receptionist on duty. They knocked on the door to the examination room, and Dr. Florentine looked up from Bianca's body.

"It's the same guy as the Ro case," he said in a matter-of-fact way. "I found another cube where the heart should be." He held up a plastic bag with the cube in it. "It says February."

Richard looked at Danny. "That guy from the holistic

store hasn't come back to us about the other one; maybe we should pay him another visit."

Danny nodded. "Let me take a picture of the cube. Anything else, Doc?" he asked as he took out his phone.

Florentine shook his head. "Surgical precision, but it was the shot to her head that killed her, a hunting rifle."

"Just like Donovan," Richard mused. "Okay, thanks, Doc. Send the report over once you're ready."

They left and headed back to the station. They didn't even bother going in; there were leads to follow.

Danny got into his car and left straightaway, pulling into traffic after punching the address for the salon into his GPS. Traffic was busy in the city center, so he waited patiently as he edged forward, hoping Richard was having better luck than him.

Finding parking was another mission once he found the salon; he had to park three blocks away and walk down the main street, dodging idiot drivers who didn't stop at the traffic lights. He only had to flash his badge when they yelled at him for them to back off.

When he reached the salon, he had worked up a sweat and mopped at his face with his sleeve. He entered and looked around. There was no one at the front desk; everyone seemed busy with a client. A teenager saw him and excused herself from her client to come over to him.

"Hi, sir, can I help you? We don't normally do gentlemen's cuts because there's a barber nearby."

Danny showed her his badge. "I need to speak to the owner."

Another blonde woman excused herself from her client and approached them. "I've got this, Mel," she turned to Danny as Mel left, "How can I help you, Officer?"

"Detective Cox," Danny extended his hand, and she shook it. "I need to know if you recently had an appointment with someone named Bianca Pike? Can you check your records?"

"Julia," she said. "And I don't need to check our records, Bianca is a great client, and we helped her two days ago. We even gave her a dress for her birthday."

Danny was taking down notes. "Do you know where she would have gone after she was done here?"

"Why? What has happened? Is she okay?" Julia asked, frowning.

Danny sighed. "Ma'am, Bianca's body was found in Midtown this morning; we're just trying to piece together as much information as possible."

Julia's eyes widened, and then tears formed. "Oh lord, she was the nicest person. Always tipped and always had a kind word... Yes, well...I kind of know what she was doing that day. I thought she was crazy, but she was adamant."

Danny watched her closely. "What was crazy?"

"She'd been chatting to this guy Wayne for a couple of weeks, even considered him her boyfriend, and her birthday was the first time they were meeting. I don't know where he was taking her or anything, but those were her plans. She even said she was going to wear the blue dress we bought her."

"Blue dress" Danny asked.

"Yes, why?"

"Because she was found in a red dress," Danny explained. "Is there anything else you can think of that could help?"

"She met him on a dating app, that new one. Hooked, I think it's called. Mel, what's that app called?"

They hadn't realized the whole salon had gone silent as they listened to the conversation; two people had tears streaming down their faces. Mel was shivering.

"Yes, it's called Hooked. Her username was Pinkili-cious220," Mel said. "We chatted on there sometimes and compared guys."

Danny wrote down the information and nodded. "Anything else?"

Julia went quiet, looking off to the side. "Her whole life was on that phone, so if you can find it, you'll prob-ably find a lot more information."

Danny took out a business card. "If anyone can think of anything that could help me track this Wayne down, please give me a call."

"I have his username," Mel said quietly.

Danny turned to her quickly. "Can you give it to me? Maybe I can contact the app developers to trace him."

Mel took out her phone, and after searching for a while, she frowned. "His profile has been deactivated, but wait, I have a screenshot from Bianca." She tinkered on her phone again and then came over. "It's HunterI1."

Danny wrote it down and gave her a small smile. "That really helps a lot." He looked at Julia. "If you think of anything, contact me."

"We will. We'll try our best to remember any details that could help," Julia said, her throat cracking slightly.

"I'm so sorry for your loss," Danny said before leaving and going back to his car. He called Richard once there and put him on speaker phone as he drove. "Did you find anything?" he asked.

Richard sighed. "Clean place, healthy girl, but no clues as to what she was doing that day other than she had a meal."

Danny sighed. "Well, I have the username for an app of a guy she was going on a date with; it might be our guy. We need a warrant to get records from the Hooked app."

"That could take days, Danny, you know how these tech giants are." Danny could hear Richard climbing into his car.

"We still need to do it; it's a chance to track him." Danny stopped at a red light. "Meet me at that holistic store; let's give Malik another talk."

"Got you," Richard said. "See you there." He dropped the call.

Danny knew the way already, driving the fastest way he could, and pulled up outside the store. It was in a quieter part of the city, so there was more parking here. He only had to wait twenty minutes before Richard was pulling into a parking spot two spaces away.

He climbed out of the car and met Richard at the door for the store; Danny led him in, a bell jingling as they entered.

Malik was a pale, skinny, tall Wiccan man they had questioned about the January cube a month ago. He had promised to see if he could source where it came from, but they hadn't heard from him, despite leaving him messages.

"Detectives, I'm afraid you've wasted your trip. I have no new information for you." He had a scratchy but deepish voice.

Danny rested his hands on the glass counter, despite the sign that said don't touch it. "Malik, I don't believe you even looked."

"I don't work for the cops," he smiled brightly, "I can help if I want to."

Before Danny could respond, Richard put a hand on his arm, and Danny moved back so Richard could move forward.

"I get you don't like cops, but there's been another murder," he explained.

"I don't see how it's my problem?" Malik cocked an eyebrow.

"You can help us willingly," Richard said. "Or we'll do regular surprise drug busts on your store and customers."

Malik crossed his arms. "I don't know what you're talking about."

"I know when I smell weed, Malik," Richard crossed his own arms, mocking the younger man. "Your customers won't want to visit if the cops keep busting at your store and arresting them. I'm sure word will get around quickly."

Malik glowered at him, and Danny stepped forward with his phone in his hand. "There is a second cube that says February and has a stone in it; we're waiting for the coroner to identify it."

Malik looked at the picture and scoffed, "It's amethyst, February's birth stone. This is clearly from a collection."

"Can you trace who sells the collection and from where? Do you have contacts?"

Malik eyed them out a moment. "It'll take some time, there's a lot of holistic stores, but I'll do what I can do."

"Don't leave us hanging too long," Richard said with a cheeky smile. "We'll wait to hear from you."

Malik frowned as Danny and Richard left the store.

"Hunting rifle, the username has hunter in it..." Danny mused as they stood outside his car. "Something tells me we have a serial killer who likes hunting humans."

"What's his angle, though?" Richard asked.

"I don't know, Rich," Danny said. "I don't know, but we're going to find out."

CHAPTER 5

2012 - 13 Years Old

Hunter woke up to the cold steel of a knife pressed against his throat. His eyes darted up to Father hovering over him.

"Good, you're awake. Let's go."

There was no room to argue as Father withdrew the blade, and Hunter got up.

"Dress in casual wear. I'm taking you to the city," Father explained.

"We never go to the city." Hunter looked confused as he pulled out jeans, a shirt, and a dark hoodie.

"Are you questioning me?" Father asked from the doorway.

"No, sir," Hunter said quickly.

His body still recalled the lashings he'd gotten a few days earlier. Father didn't like being questioned; they lived by his rules and his rules alone. Otherwise, other people would interfere in their lives, probably take Hunter away from him or hurt him or worse. Father had told him how horrible people were; he'd grown up learning about them.

He dressed quickly and followed Father downstairs.

"I have a gift for you. I want you to treat it with the same respect you give me," Father said.

He held out a box, and Hunter took it, setting it on the table and opening up the cardboard. Inside, nestled in some brown paper, was a long hunting knife with a sheath. Hunter took it out and admired it.

"You are to protect yourself with it. Keep it on you whenever you leave the cabin."

"Yes, Father, thank you." Hunter tied the sheath around his leg, and the knife fit snuggly at the top; with his oversized hoodie, he could hide the blade that way.

Father put on his own knife and a long jacket. "Tonight, you're going to practice what I've been teaching you about quick kills." Father handed Hunter a pair of gloves. "Put these on and never take them off, at any time, until we're back."

Hunter put on the gloves and waited for his next instructions. Father passed him a hat. "Pull his low so that no camera can catch your face."

Hunter pulled it on, and Father did the same with

his cap and gloves before leading the way to the front door. "Come."

Hunter followed Father to his truck and climbed into the passenger side. Father started the truck, and they began their drive to the main road, using a back door service road that was supposed to be out of service. It was only used by them.

"The first thing you need to know is to lure the person into a false sense of security. Sometimes this will take you out of your comfort zone. You have to be prepared to do whatever it takes to obtain your prey."

Hunter stared straight ahead and nodded. "Yes, Father."

"I want you to really listen because once we get there, I'm leaving you on your own to do this. Do you remember what a prostitute is, Hunter?"

He seldom used Hunter's name, and when he did, Hunter got the shivers. He still didn't look at Father, observing the forest around them for potential threats.

"A prostitute is someone disgusting who sells their body and drugs or sells their body for drugs. They are a sub-species to us. They don't deserve to roam the land. They are non-human."

"That's correct, you remembered. You forgot, however, to mention that they can be either male or female. Why is this important?"

"Males could be a bigger threat, especially if they work out to keep up appearances." Hunter felt excited as they got onto the main road that led toward the rescue center. It was an hour's drive there, and then they would join the main highway to the city.

"Good, you've been studying hard. Tonight you are going to use money to lure a prostitute to an alleyway, and you're going to slash her throat and bring me her ear as proof. If you fail to do this, don't bother to come back to me at all."

"Yes, Father," Hunter said quietly.

Father reached over and slapped the back of his head, "Don't mutter, speak up."

"Yes, Father," Hunter said with more confidence. "Sorry."

Father glanced at him and then back at the road. The rest of the trip they spent in absolute silence. The truck didn't have a radio to play music, and Father didn't like to be spoken to unless he had asked you to speak. So Hunter kept his eyes trained on the road.

Father turned onto the main highway; the lights from the other cars made Hunter squint. He was only used to natural lighting, not the bright headlights of cars.

"Open your eyes properly," Father growled. "Don't be a despicable little weakling. It's just light."

Hunter forced his eyes open, even though they teared up slightly; he tried to hide it from Father.

They drove through the suburbs and finally reached the city. Father seemed to be following the signs that pointed to downtown. Hunter had studied the city and knew it was an unsavory section of the town that most 'good' people avoided. Drugs, prostitution, murder... poor people had taken it over.

Father pulled into a parking lot for a restaurant that had already closed for the night. He turned to Hunter. "What is your task?"

"Lure a prostitute into an alley, slash her throat, and bring you her ear as proof."

"Or?"

"Or don't bother coming back at all," Hunter said, swallowing slightly.

"Don't be afraid," Father said. "Fear is weakness. You are not weak. Go, don't get caught or seen."

Hunter climbed out of the truck and walked down the main street. There were a lot of people about, and it made Hunter nervous, but no one seemed to pay him any mind. Maybe it was because he was tall for his age. Father had once said he looked older than he was, which he could use to his advantage.

He wanted to make his choice a younger woman; they would be less experienced and wouldn't see his attack coming.

He saw several prostitutes were standing in groups of two or three. He found an alley and stood just inside it, leaning nonchalantly against the wall.

Hunter watched as the prostitutes were slowly collected by their customers. He spotted one dark-haired girl who was with an older woman. He watched them most of all.

The older woman was finally collected and left the young girl by herself; the girl couldn't be more than fifteen. Hunter pushed off the wall and approached her slowly. She saw him and smiled brightly.

"Looking for a good time, honey?" she asked with a flirtatious smile; her eyes, however, told a different, rather drugged story.

Hunter nodded. "In the alley back there," he commented, turning and walking away.

"What you want? I'll give you a blow for twenty."

"That's fine." Hunter led her down the dark alley, making sure that there was no one else there.

She waited for him to prop himself against the wall before she slowly got to her knees, she lifted his hoodie to get to his jeans, and he grabbed his knife, pulling it out quickly and stabbing her in the throat.

Her gasp was a wet gurgling one as he withdrew the blade. He then drew the knife across her throat, blood spurting on him. She dropped to the floor clutching her throat, the light slowly fading from her eyes.

He knelt beside her head and cut off her ear; it was a bit difficult, and the metallic smell of blood assaulted his senses. Somehow human blood smelled different from animal blood to him.

He pocketed her ear and sheathed his knife. He looked down and realized he had large dark bloodstains on him. He looked around, there was no one about, but someone might see him on the street.

Hunter didn't think he should run because that would definitely attract attention. Luckily his hoodie was dark, so he pulled it as low as it went, and it covered most of the blood.

He walked down the alley and out, walking confidently back toward the parking lot where Father was parked. He hadn't moved; he was just sitting there, reading a book.

Hunter climbed into the truck and waited.

"Do you have it?" Father asked.

Hunter pulled out the ear and passed it to him.

"You've done well, messy but well. Did anyone see you?"

"No, sir," Hunter said. "I made sure no one saw me."

Father started the truck and pulled out of the parking space.

"This is our calling, Hunter. This is what we do. We purge the world and remind them how fleeting time is." Father stared straight ahead at traffic. "You passed a great test today. You'll one day be ready to do this on your own. Do you accept this?"

"Yes, Father, I look forward to it," Hunter commented.

Father pulled onto the main highway and drove them back to their hidden cabin.

. . .

2021 - PRESENT DAY

March - Timothy

The children were excited, all eleven boys talking to each other as they sat on the bus on their way to their camping trip.

It wasn't exactly how Timothy had expected to spend his birthday, but it would be fun just the same, and once they were back, he would go out for a nice dinner with his friends and family to make up for it. It just came with the territory of being a scout master.

The bus pulled into the parking lot at the east entrance of the forest they would be camping in, and Timothy got off the bus first. "Remember to stick with your buddy. Eric, you're with James and Hilton as buddies, don't forget."

The troop left the bus and grabbed their camping supplies, and Timothy led them into the woods. They would be camping for two days and would be working on trapping, knots, fire-making, raft building, and a whole lot of other activities that he and the other scout masters had planned.

They started to hike through the forest, camp master Scott leading them in song as they walked to keep their spirits up. It wasn't a long hike; it only took them thirty minutes to reach the campsite, and then they broke off to set up their tents and collect wood for the fire pit.

The boys were more than excited as they finished

their tents and broke off into small groups to complete exercises with the three different scout masters.

Timothy took the four boys he had with him down to the river. The scout masters had been down the day before to set out all the supplies they would need; they often held camps in this area because it was safe.

Timothy pointed to the rope and wood. "We're going to create a raft and see if you'll be able to float on them. You must each make your own; don't forget the correct knots to use."

He went between them as they worked so he could help them and observe them to see if they earned their badges. They would have a ceremony at the end of the camp to award the new badges, and he hoped to hand every boy each activities badge; he loved it when his kids excelled.

For most of the day, they rotated the kids through the various activities, the three scout masters remaining at the stations and the children moving through them until they'd done all the activities for that day. They built their campfire and sat around it as the boys ate the packed dinners that were supplied.

Scott sat next to Timothy. "You can head out."

"Sorry?" Timothy asked.

Scott smiled. "Most of the activities were done today; I'll record the badge ceremony for you. Go home and enjoy your birthday."

Timothy was a bit flustered, but Scott put a hand on

his shoulder. "Please, you do so much for us. At least let us do this for you."

The boys started talking about Timothy going home as well, telling him they would be fine.

Timothy smiled warmly. "Thanks, guys. I hope you have a fun weekend."

He grabbed his rucksack, and Scott called, "I'll bring your tent back with me; don't stress about it."

"Thanks," Timothy said. "Bye, everyone."

Everyone chorused their goodbyes, and Timothy headed off, his flashlight in hand as he navigated the footpath back to the bus.

He had been walking for about twenty minutes when he stopped suddenly. He could have sworn he'd heard a voice in the distance. He strained his ears. There it was again; it sounded like someone his age calling for help.

Timothy glanced around, thinking maybe he should get Scott but then decided he'd be fine; he had first aid training and a kit in his bag. He left the path and headed for the voice. He called out.

"Hello? Hello, can you hear me? Keep calling. I'm coming."

As Timothy got closer, he realized he was mistaken; the person actually sounded younger than him. He hurried forward, stumbling through the brush. He came into a clearing and swept his flashlight around. The voice was clear here. He saw something glinting in the grass ahead and slowly approached it, keeping his light trained on it. He knelt down.

It was a speaker, and the voice was coming from it. He frowned. "What the..."

He couldn't finish the sentence as the bullet entered his head at his temple and flew out the other side. He fell to the ground, and Hunter came into the clearing. He switched the speaker off and looked down at Timothy.

Timothy's eyes were still open, staring straight ahead. Hunter put away the speaker and pulled Timothy over his shoulder, rucksack and all. He turned and made his way through the forest back to his truck, where he deposited Timothy's body in the bed.

Hunter climbed in and started the truck, pulling off and making his way slowly through the trees. He couldn't deny that he felt a deep sense of satisfaction that everything was going according to plan. Father always said not to be arrogant, but surely he could take pride in the fact he was doing a good job.

Hunter wondered if Father was proud. He could never tell; Father was very stern and never showed his emotions, something Hunter still needed to control fully. He could almost get it right, up until he was disappointed; his disappointment always showed on his face.

He pulled up to the cabin and climbed out. He hoisted Timothy's body over his shoulder and took him downstairs. He knew Father wouldn't be back for a few days, so he got to work immediately. He cut Timothy's scout uniform from his body, then his underwear until he was naked on the gurney.

Hunter took a moment to examine Timothy in detail. He was well-toned, clearly an outdoorsman, and yet such an easy kill. Hunter felt that it was almost unfair and not sporting how he took out these idiots.

It was so easy for him. They were so trusting, so noble, so naive. Hunter was thankful he had been raised in a realistic house where they always spoke the truth.

He changed into his scrubs and put on his gloves before picking up his scalpel. He started cutting the chest open; he used a bone saw to get through his sternum before carefully cutting out and removing the heart. He added it to the available jar on the tray next to him and closed the jar.

He wiped his hands and opened the wooden box, retrieving the third cube. He placed it carefully in the chest cavity where the heart was and started to close Timothy's chest.

Once done, he dressed Timothy as though he was going for a jog, lacing up trainers on his feet and putting a cap on his head.

Hunter stood back and admired his handiwork. He smiled softly, then whipped around to grab Father's hand before it could strike him on the back of the head.

He dropped his hand. "Sorry, Father, I didn't know it was you."

Father looked at Timothy and then at Hunter, waiting.

"I wasn't expecting you for a few days," Hunter said quietly. "I hope you are pleased with my work today."

Father backhanded him across the face. "You looked so arrogant just now, smiling at this corpse as though no one could do this as well as you. You're replaceable, Hunter. Everyone is. Go to the shed."

Hunter stripped off the scrubs and deposited them in a basket near the stairs. He then stripped the rest of his clothes off and folded them, carrying them upstairs and setting them on the sideboard at the top of the stairs before going to the shed naked. Father didn't have to tell him what to do. He had been arrogant; he deserved this.

He got the steps and stepped up, looping his hands through the worn leather straps. Father took the steps away, and Hunter dangled there, holding himself as his muscles bulged.

Father had, long ago, upped his game from a simple leather belt. He picked up a cat of nine tails, holding it tightly in his hand.

"What is the most important rule?" he asked calmly.

"Don't get arrogant; arrogance leads to sloppiness which leads to mistakes."

"And?"

"Mistakes get you caught," Hunter said, bracing himself.

He stopped counting after the twentieth time he was struck; he could feel the blood trickling down his body.

Father set the steps back, and Hunter climbed down. As he made his way to the door, Father moved in front of him. "Hunter, I do this for you, son. Like my father did for me and his father before him. For twelve generations, our family has cleaned this world in our own way. Soon you will be out on your own, and I will find a quiet place to rest, but you need to remember your lessons so I can do that."

"Yes, Father, I will do better." Hunter looked at him; they were an equal height now, and Father nodded.

"Go shower. You need to take that body tonight."

CHAPTER 6

"Don't forget, she has a gymnastics meet tonight that we promised to watch," Lexie said as she kissed Danny on his way out the door.

Danny kissed her back. "I have to do the farewell for Jerome, but once that's done, I'll be right over. Might be a few minutes late."

"Just don't forget, Danny." Lexie smiled.

Danny left and got into his car just as his phone rang. He glanced at the caller ID and answered, "Richard?"

"Another body, this time in Newlands Park."

"Shit, same guy?" Danny asked.

Richard paused. "We think so, the body is posed, and he was shot in the head. I'm already here."

"I'll be there shortly," Danny promised, hanging up.

He turned his sirens on and pulled out quickly, navigating his way through the traffic that moved out of his way. It took him twenty-five minutes to arrive; Richard was leaning against his car waiting.

Danny climbed out of his car and went to him.

"Where is the body?" Danny asked.

Richard stood up. "This way," he said, walking down a joggers' path.

They reached the crime scene tape, and a technician gave them booties and gloves before allowing them under the tape. Richard led him over to the bench where there was a body of a young man reading a newspaper, wire holding his body in place. He had a cap next to him.

"Someone stopped to check on him, pulled his cap off and saw the bullet entry and exit wounds, and called the cops," Richard explained. "I have two officers questioning her now."

Danny reached for the man's shirt, tugging the collar down slightly. "He's been opened up; it is the same guy."

Richard sighed and looked up and down the path. "Did you see the news this morning?"

Danny shook his head, standing straight.

"Someone spilled the MO; the news is calling this killer Stones because he leaves stones in their chest." Richard rolled his eyes. "These news outlets need a freaking life."

"They're going to put pressure on the captain, who's

going to put pressure on us to solve this," Danny pointed out.

Richard nodded. "I know. Any ideas?"

Danny shook his head. "No, bullets are generic hunting bullets you can buy anywhere. Anything from Malik about those stones?"

Richard sighed. "I actually spoke to him two days ago; he said he found the distributor. He's just trying to get a list of who they sold them to. Apparently it was a collector's edition, so there's that."

"They're not being killed where their bodies are dumped. We need to figure out if they're being killed in the same place," Danny suggested.

"Well, Donovan was killed on a hike, and our guys have tried going down all the hiking paths and haven't found anything of interest."

Danny led him back toward their cars. "Basically, he was hunted down in the woods, though. Maybe what we need to do is check the parking lots of the different entrances to the woods for Bianca's car because they still haven't found it."

Richard looked thoughtful. "That's an idea. We can do that today."

"I'll take the north and east entrances, and you can take the south and west entrances," Danny offered.

Richard gave him a thumbs-up, and they both got in their cars and pulled out of the parking lot, driving in opposite directions.

Danny's mind spun in circles as he drove. He didn't know how, but he was so sure that Bullseye was connected to this case. It wasn't usual for a serial killer to change their MO, but it wasn't unheard of. He drummed his fingers on his steering wheel as he stopped at a light.

"What have you got to do with this case, Waters," he muttered to himself.

Once he reached the north entrance to the forest, he got out and looked for any Mini Coopers. It was a large parking lot, so it took him a while to walk around it before he returned to his vehicle, texting Richard to let him know he'd had no luck and was moving on.

A few minutes later, Richard texted him back and let him know there was nothing at the west entrance because it had been closed up for months.

Danny stopped to put gas in his car and grab a coffee, going over the evidence in his mind. Soon he was back on the road. The actual entrances weren't at the exact north, west, east, and south points of the forest—the forest was huge—but it was just how they had been labeled. Danny was about twenty minutes away from the east entrance when Richard called him.

"We've got it. It's at the south entrance. I've called a tech team here already," Richard said, sounding out of breath.

"Something happen?" Danny asked. "It'll take me a while to get there."

Richard took a deep breath and chuckled, "No, I'm fine. I just ran across the lot to the car when I saw it. Really need to get back in shape."

"Dad bods are a thing now," Danny laughed.

"That's for you, mate. I'm no one's dad. Don't worry about coming here. Go back to the station. Once the tech team has been here and I've gone over the scene, I'll meet you there."

Danny agreed and dropped the call. He did a U-turn and started back the way he had come, glad he wasn't driving all the way to the south entrance.

Once he reached the station, he had to get a parking spot right at the back of the lot and walk across it to the entrance.

The front of the station was buzzing with reporters, and as soon as they saw him, they ran for him. He held his hands up and said, "I have no comment, don't even bother."

They shot their questions at him anyway, and he just quietly made his way through the crowd until he got to the back part of the station, through a door, and into the detectives' area.

A few cops were busy arranging decorations in boxes, and Danny made his way over to them.

"Did someone order a cake for the party?" he asked.

The captain came up behind him. "Don't worry; everything is organized for Jerome's party. Tell me what we know about our latest victim?"

Danny turned to him. "Nothing much. There was no identification on the body. We'll have to wait for Florentine to confirm the victim belongs to the same guy, but I'm sure of it; he had cuts that show he's been opened up. On a positive note, we've found the second victim's car."

Captain Baker raised an eyebrow. "Where?"

"The south entrance to the forest which leads me to believe that both the first and second victim was killed somewhere on the edge of the forest."

"Solid lead," the captain responded. "Keep me updated, Danny. The media are crucifying us over this. They're bringing up the fact Bullseye escaped, and now another serial killer is running around killing and posing people."

Danny nodded. "You got it, boss." He went back to his desk to work on some paperwork while waiting for Richard.

By the time Richard arrived back at the station, it was almost time to leave for Jerome's party. Danny looked at his partner as he sat at his desk, looking flustered.

"They'll let us know if there's anything in the car that can help us," Richard said. "I tried walking around the area, but I didn't really find anything that could help. I'm going to ask the captain to send a team out there to comb the area and see if they can find anything."

Danny ran a hand over his head. "Captain wants this

solved. The media are on his case. You know the mayor won't be far behind."

"If he's not already," Richard pointed out. "Ready for the party?"

Danny nodded and stood, putting his jacket on. The bar was down the road from the station, so they walked there with a few other detectives attending.

The bar had been decked out with decorations, banners, and balloons, and there was a huge tiered cake at the end of the bar.

They all ordered drinks and sat around, waiting for Jerome to make his way to them. He was stopping and talking with each little cluster of detectives—making his way around the bar.

The cake was handed out, and Jerome had to pause milling about to give a speech. They toasted him, and he finally made his way to Danny and Richard. Jerome sat down in the booth with them and smiled.

"I'm going to miss you pains the ass the most," he chuckled, sipping his beer.

Danny snorted into his beer. "Not as much as we'll miss you, old man."

Richard grinned; he had a whiskey in front of him. "So, Jerome, what is it?"

"What is what?"

"The case?" Richard asked. "The one case you never got to solve that you wish you had; everyone has one."

Danny raised an eyebrow. "What a depressing topic, Rich."

"What?" Richard asked. "Everyone does have one."

Jerome sighed and nodded, smiling a sad smile. "Yeah, there was one. A kidnapping I worked. Never found the kid or the body. If I could solve one last case, I'd want it to be that one."

Danny sat back. "We all have that one case."

Richard looked at him knowingly, and Jerome chuckled, "We all know yours, Danny."

Danny smiled at him. "I'm going to catch that son of a bitch before my career is over if it kills me."

"Don't let Lexie hear you say that," Jerome teased. "I think she'll be mighty pissed."

Danny smiled again. "Let's just keep it here between us."

Jerome spoke with them for a little while longer before moving on to the next group. Richard's phone rang, and he excused himself to take the call outside. Danny sighed, staring into his beer.

"That was the morgue," Richard sat back down. "They can't identify the guy at all. They tried everything, but it seems like he isn't on the DMV or any other system we have."

"He does look a bit young. Maybe he didn't get around to getting his license," Danny suggested.

Richard sipped on his whiskey, and they fell into a

comfortable silence, each detective thinking about the case and a way to identify the new victim.

"Media," they both said suddenly, and Danny nodded. "We'll get a picture and release it to the media and see if anyone recognizes him. It'll be the fastest way to get a name."

Richard stood up. "I'll get the approval from Baker and organize it."

Danny stood up. "I'll come with."

Richard downed his whiskey. "It's okay. You go home. I'll sort it out."

Danny paled, and Richard paused. "What?"

Danny looked at his watch. "Shit. Cleo had a gymnastics thing today that I was supposed to be at almost an hour ago, and it's gonna take me at least forty-five minutes to get there."

"Better hurry," Richard said, shooing him out the door.

Danny downed his beer and rushed out the door, calling bye to Jerome as he passed. He practically ran back to the station and got into his car, pulling out quickly. He tried to drive as patiently as he could to the school, but even with a slightly heavier foot on the gas, it still took him thirty-five minutes to get there.

As he walked toward the gym door, it opened, and people spilled out. Danny groaned and stepped aside to let the people pass. He waited, scanning the crowd. He saw Lexie and waved her down. She gave him a stern look and shook her head.

Cleo was next to her, and Danny approached them. "Cleo, I'm so sorry..." he started to say.

Cleo walked past him and toward Lexie's car.

"Cleo!" Danny called after her.

"Don't bother, she's pissed, and she has every right to be. She never asks you to come to meets unless they're important, and you miss the one where she came first." Lexie shook her head.

Danny put a hand on her arm. "I'm sorry, I did completely forget. It's been a day. Please forgive me."

"I don't need to forgive you, Danny," Lexie said sadly. "It's Cleo you need to convince."

She kissed his cheek and headed for her car, where Cleo was waiting. Danny sighed and walked back to his car. He knew Cleo wouldn't speak to him for a while because of this.

He followed Lexie home and parked behind her. As he climbed out, he thought he would try anyway.

"Cleo? Honey, please let me explain," he said as she walked past.

Cleo walked into the house and slammed the door shut behind her. Lexie shook her head. "She'll get over it eventually."

"It was a genuine mistake, love," Danny moaned. "I feel like shit."

"You should," Lexie smiled, leading him into the house. "I'm going to get started on dinner."

He let her go and went upstairs to shower and change.

DANNY WALKED INTO THE STATION THE FOLLOWING DAY TO find the captain and a few detectives watching the news on the television set against the wall. There was a picture of their victim shown with the news anchor asking anyone who may know him to come forward and identify him.

Danny sat at his desk after putting his gun and badge in his drawer and watched the news report as well.

"The police still have no leads on this killer known only as Stones by locals, and the people of the city are questioning whether or not the department can keep them safe. This is the second active serial killer in the city in two years. The killer known as Bullseye, or Jack Waters, escaped a prison transport on his way to maximum holding last year. Detectives have yet to trace his whereabouts and cannot even confirm if it's him committing these murders as well."

The captain muted the television and turned to look at Danny, who held his hands up. "I'll be down at the morgue as soon as Richard arrives."

Baker looked at him for a moment before going to his office and shutting the door. It wasn't long after that when Richard walked in and set a coffee on Danny's table. "Morning, sunshine, how much shit are you in?"

"Don't sit. We need to go get the report from the morgue." Danny retrieved his gun and badge and picked up his coffee, leading Richard out. "And I'm in deep shit with Cleo."

Richard smiled knowingly. "This is why…"

"You don't have kids," Danny finished the sentence as he unlocked the car. "And you know what, I still wouldn't trade with you."

They pulled out of the parking lot, and Danny drove them to the morgue, their police scanner the only sound in the car.

Florentine looked up as they walked in. "We have March, gentleman. It's definitely your guy."

He pointed to a plastic bag that held a cube in it. Richard looked at it closely. "I've been reading up on these birthstones; this must be aquamarine."

Danny looked at Florentine. "Please tell me you have something we can use."

"He was very big on the outdoors judging by the dirt under his nails and his tan. He also has rough hands, so he worked with them. Unfortunately, I don't have much else. The clothes are just standard items you could get at any general store, and there's no dirt under the shoes, so they must be new."

"Wait, was there dirt under any of the other victims' shoes?" Danny asked.

Florentine looked at him over his glasses. "Actually, no, there wasn't."

"They aren't being posed in the clothes they were in. He's dressing them up," Danny turned to Richard. "And I bet this guy was killed on his birthday like Bianca and Donovan."

"But how does he know what their birthdays are and where they'll be?" Richard asked, looking at the body.

Danny put his hands on his hips. "There must be something that connects them. We need to find what that is. We need to first identify this guy and then see what he shares with the other two."

"Didn't Bianca meet the killer on that app?" Richard asked. "Maybe they're all on there. I know those dating apps show your birth date and location."

"How would you know?" Danny asked curiously, raising an eyebrow.

Richard snorted. "Because I use them to pick up chicks, Danny, how else?"

Danny shook his head. "I have no words. Doc, if you can, please get us that report as soon as possible."

Florentine nodded. "The captain has already called, so has the mayor. These murders take priority." He sounded jaded, but Danny didn't have time for that.

He led Richard out of the building, and they stood by

the car for a moment. Danny leaned against the hood, his arms crossed over his chest.

Richard sighed and crossed his arms. "No idea where to go now?"

"None at all," Danny admitted. "We need to figure out where these Stones originated from."

"Well then, I know exactly where we're going," Richard smiled. "Let's go visit our friend Malik."

Danny shrugged. "It's not far from here. Let's walk."

They took off down the street.

They opened the store door, and the bell jingled. They were surprised to see a rather goth-looking girl behind the counter.

"Hello, we're looking for Malik," Richard said.

Malik came out from the back room. "I told you I haven't found anything out yet."

Richard sighed. "Malik, we really need this list. There's been another victim."

"You're cops?" the girl asked, looking at Malik curiously.

Danny stepped forward. "Yes, Malik is trying to get us a customer list of a limited edition item."

Out of nowhere, the girl slapped the back of Malik's head and looked at the two detectives. "I apologize if my husband has been a bit of an ass; he does that to cops. His father was a deadbeat and a patrolman."

Danny tried to suppress his smile. "It's okay. What's your name?"

"I don't like my real name; everyone calls me Raven." She held out a hand and first shook Danny's, then Richard's. "What do you need? I'll get it for you."

"Raven," Malik started to say, but she glared at him, and he fell silent. Malik sighed. "I already have it," he muttered. "I'll go get it."

"Thanks, Malik," Richard said cheerily. "And thank you, Raven. I really appreciate the assistance."

"If I had known, I would have gotten it to you sooner, but I've been out of state visiting my mother." She gave them a sad smile. "The victim... Are you talking about that guy they had on the news?"

"Yes, we need to identify him. Hopefully, a family member or friend sees the news and comes forward."

"What list did you need from Malik?" Raven asked.

"The killer is leaving these birth stones in cubes... with the victims. I need to trace them down to see if we can catch the guy." Richard stood straight as Malik walked back in.

"Well, I hope you get him soon," Raven said as Malik handed over the thumb drive.

"Thank you for your help, Raven, and you, Malik." Danny looked at him pointedly. "If we need more information about the stones, we'll pop in."

"Anytime," Raven offered.

The detectives left the store and went to pick up the car and go back to the station. Once there, they plugged the thumb drive into Danny's computer. After it was scanned for viruses, they opened the spreadsheet.

"There are at least a thousand names here," Danny frowned, "This is going to take forever."

Richard nodded. "Split it up. We'll get some guys to follow up on them. See if anyone is missing any cubes from their collection."

Danny nodded. "It could take weeks; I don't think we have that kind of time."

"Any other suggestions then?" Richard looked down at him from where he stood.

Danny shook his head. "I didn't say we mustn't do it. I just think we need to find another angle to work as well."

Richard put a hand on his shoulder. "We're doing everything we can, Danny. We're going to catch this guy."

"How many people will be dead before we do?" Danny asked, looking up at him.

CHAPTER 7

2010 - 11 YEARS OLD

THE NIGHTS HAD GROWN COLDER, AND HUNTER HAD harvested the last of the summer vegetables and started their winter crop. Father had overseen his work, directing him from a chair at the edge of their little garden. Hunter would sweat under his jacket, liquid dripping down his face, his neck, and down his back.

He worked well into the afternoon before Father allowed him to shower and change. He came downstairs in a tracksuit pants and sweatshirt, going to sit at the table to have his lunch. While he ate his sandwich, he listened to the radio, enjoying the classical music it offered.

Once he had washed his dishes, Father came

upstairs from the basement. "Get dressed warmly; we're going into the forest tonight."

Hunter looked at him curiously. "Why?"

"Are you questioning me, boy?"

Hunter quickly shook his head and made his way upstairs to change. He sat on his bed and read a book while he waited. After what felt like an hour had passed, his door opened, and Father stood there, dressed warmly.

"Come," he said simply.

Hunter set his book down and followed Father downstairs and to his truck. They drove into the dark forest with only Father's headlights showing them the way. Hunter wasn't sure how long they drove for, but it felt long; he had started to drift off.

Suddenly Father was shaking him awake, and he sat up quickly. "I'm sorry."

Father looked ahead. "It's time we make sure you've been studying your astronomy."

"Do you want me to name the stars?" Hunter asked curiously.

Father frowned. "Get out; I'm going home. You're going to navigate your way there using the stars."

Hunter looked out at the forest and then at Father. "What about predators?"

"Are you afraid to do what I've asked?" Father looked at him coldly.

Hunter shook his head despite feeling terrified.

Father had left him in the woods before for a few hours, but he was always armed.

He climbed out of the truck and stood by while Father drove off. He wondered if he could run fast enough to follow Father home, but he knew what kind of punishment he would get if he did that.

No, this was a test that he needed to pass. He looked up at the sky, trying to figure out which stars were which and which direction he had to head. Hunter wished he had paid more attention to the direction Father had driven out because that would help him get back. He was an idiot for falling asleep.

He heard the rush of the river and secretly rejoiced. He knew his way home from the river. It flowed from the western mountain down east. He walked in that direction.

He walked for some time before suddenly coming out on a noticeably flat, straight piece of land. He frowned; in the moonlight, he could see it stretched far. That's when he realized Father had dropped him near the service road.

He panicked momentarily because he had never been in this direction before. Father always took him deeper into the woods, not closer to other people. He ducked behind a tree and looked around; he could still hear the river. It sounded like it was down the road to his right.

He looked up at the stars, and knowing which way

was west and east, he managed to figure out where Polaris was. Once he found it, he looked around. It would be difficult to follow it through the trees; he was sure he had to go in a northeastern direction.

He turned to face the correct way and started walking, trying to keep an eye out for clear areas where he could check the stars. He was sure he was going in the right direction and walked confidently, keeping an ear out for any would-be predators.

After what felt like forever, he heard a noise and ducked down behind a tree. There was a snuffling sound, what could be a pig. He needed to find somewhere to hide; wild pigs were dangerous, and he didn't have any way to protect himself.

As he was about to dart out and run, the pig rounded the corner, and Hunter could see a reflective collar on it. He frowned, confused, and backed away slowly into another person who put his hands on Hunter's shoulders. Hunter tried to pull away.

"Easy, kid, easy. I'm not going to hurt you."

Hunter whipped out of his hands and backed up against the tree.

"Are you lost?" the older man asked. "Piglet and I were just hunting for truffles. I can take you to the police station so they can find your parents."

Hunter eyed him out, glancing around to see where he could run to, panicked that the man would force him to go with him.

The guy kept his hands held up. "I'm not going to hurt you," he promised. "My name is Mike; I'm a chef in the city. How did you get out here? Is your family camping in this forest?"

When Hunter didn't answer, Mike stood up straight with his hands on his hips. "Look, I can't leave you here, so come on, march on, young man. I'm taking you to the cops."

Unsure how he could resist and very frightened, Hunter allowed Mike to take his arm and lead him through the trees. Hunter felt as though he was going to cry. He tried to pull away from Mike, but he held Hunter firmly, the large sow Piglet trotting alongside them.

They hadn't gone far when Piglet suddenly dropped to the ground. Mike turned his head. "Stay here."

He walked to where Piglet was lying. "Pigs?" he whispered, kneeling.

Suddenly, he fell backward, and Hunter saw a large wound on his forehead. Hunter looked around desperately until he saw Father emerge from the trees, dressed in camouflage. Hunter wanted to run to him but remembered himself at the last possible moment.

Father was glaring at him; if looks could kill, Hunter would also be lying on the ground with Mike and Piglet. Hunter stood still, waiting for Father to reach him.

"You're weak and pathetic. This had better not happen again, or I'll take you out next time," Father growled.

Hunter sniffed and nodded.

"Are you crying, boy?" he demanded.

Hunter shook his head.

"Come, we're going home. You nearly made it back to where a bunch of people camp," Father explained. "Complete failure. You went in the wrong direction."

"I was following Polaris," Hunter pointed to the star.

Father backhanded him. "That's not Polaris; you haven't studied at all."

Hunter held his face as Father turned away and walked into the trees; he kept up as best he could, not wanting to be left behind.

He was exhausted, and his small legs were so sore from the walk he just wanted to get to bed. He was so happy when they turned into their driveway. The truck was noticeably absent; Hunter thought Father must have left it somewhere while he tracked him. Hunter walked toward the house.

"The shed," Father said, setting down his rifle and taking off his belt.

Hunter looked at him with wide eyes. "Father, I'm sorry."

"Not yet, you're not," Father said. "The shed."

Hunter walked to the shed and pulled out the steps. He undressed until he was naked before climbing the steps and then shimmied up the pole to grasp the leather straps. He looped his hands in them and dangled in mid-air.

Father removed the stairs and stood to his left. "This is something that could mean the difference between life and death for you. Failure in this is unacceptable under any circumstance. The world is unfair, and it will not be kind to you. You need to apply yourself to my teachings or choose to leave."

"I want to stay," Hunter's voice cracked.

"Then do as I say," Father said before starting to lash at Hunter's body continuously. Red welts formed everywhere he struck, but Hunter didn't whimper; he knew it would only make Father angrier.

Once done, Father pushed the stairs back, and Hunter painfully lowered himself down the pole. He got dressed and looked up at Father.

"No sleep tonight," Father said. "Go get your studies and come sit in the kitchen. You will study the remainder of the night." He turned and walked out of the shed.

Hunter lowered his head and followed him out, obeying him and going to get his materials so he could study, trying his best not to wince when he sat down on his stinging ass.

2021 - Present Day

April - Alicia and Owen

Being a twin was both the hardest thing in the world to do and also the most fun thing. You lived in your own unique world with your twin, and Alicia couldn't ask for a better brother than Owen.

No matter what happened, if they hadn't spoken in weeks or had a recent disagreement, they *always* celebrated their birthday together.

Today was no different; they'd agreed to go bar-hopping together. Every year they ended their party at their favorite bar before catching a cab back to their respective houses. It was a great night, and they always shared a major hangover the next day to prove it.

Alicia had gotten Owen a special gift because it was their thirtieth. She had ordered him signed copies of his favorite author's books. Toni Cox was hard to reach in Germany, but her trilogy books were something Owen talked about all the time. So she had ordered hardcovers especially for him, asking Toni to sign and ship them. It had cost a pretty penny, but it was so worth it to Alicia; she couldn't wait to give Owen his gift. She'd do it at breakfast the next day while they were nursing their hangovers. Tonight was for celebrating.

They both loved rock music, and tonight they were hopping from one rock bar to the next, so they could jam to all their favorite tunes. She had dressed in a small black skirt, black tights, a black off-shoulder top, and had straightened her chin-length black hair. Her final touch was the knee-high boots she put on.

She caught a cab to the first bar and waited outside for Owen and their friends. People started arriving quickly enough, and soon Owen was there in his ripped jeans, band shirt, and mohawk. They hugged tightly before shouting at each other, "Happy birthday!"

They burst out laughing and turned, leading everyone into the first bar. From there, the sky was their limit. They were both making good pay, and their friends bought drinks for them as well, so by the fifth bar, they were already quite sloshed, as were most of their friends.

By the seventh, Owen could barely stand, so Alicia called their goodbyes and stumbled with him out of the bar, standing on the side to hail a cab.

It didn't take long for one to pull up, which was surprising; there generally weren't a lot of cabs available at this time, especially in the area they were in. They were at the edge of the city in an industrial section, where the rock bars liked to be because they could make as much noise at night as they wanted.

The cab stopped, and Owen tumbled in. As soon as Alicia helped him get upright, she climbed in as well.

"Thirteen Sixth Avenue in Midtown, please," Alicia slurred at the driver. He nodded his acknowledgment and started to drive.

It would take them a while to get there, so Alicia stared out the window, her eyes drooping as Owen snored next to her.

"Please wake me when we get there," she murmured, closing her eyes.

She jolted awake, realizing her mistake. She looked at her watch; they had left the last bar almost two hours ago. She then looked around at her whereabouts; they were surrounded by trees. Panicked, Alicia shook Owen.

"Owen, wake up. We've been kidnapped," she whispered urgently, looking around for the driver.

Before Owen could mutter a response, his door opened, and blood splattered over Alicia's face as a bullet exited the side of his head and lodged into her shoulder.

She screamed as the gun aimed at her. She scrambled to get out of the car, but the door was locked. She shrieked for a moment before Hunter silenced her permanently.

Hunter got back into the driver's side and started to drive through the forest. He would dispose of the cab much later when it was safer. He had used false plates so no one could trace him, having stolen the cab three months ago.

He pulled next to his truck and looked behind him. He would use the girl for the stone; he was just the bonus. He retrieved Alicia's body out of the back and took her downstairs to the gurney. He then brought Owen down and propped him sitting against the wall.

Hunter donned his scrubs and stroked Alicia's hair out of her face before cutting her clothes off, then her underwear, then his hand hovered above her body with a scalpel in it.

He first used the scalpel to remove the bullet that had lodged into her shoulder. He sewed that up before opening her chest. Once she was wide open, he removed her heart and placed it in the jar, a larger one than the others so he could fit both hearts. He then stitched her back up and dressed her before propping her next to Owen.

Deciding to take a break, he took off the scrubs and gloves and headed upstairs. Father was sitting at the kitchen table; two bowls of steaming bear stew were waiting.

"You didn't have to wait," Hunter said quietly.

Father shook his head. "Sit, let's eat before it gets cold. You can turn the radio on."

Hunter turned on the radio and sat down; they ate to various composers' masterpieces. Once done, Hunter got up to do the dishes, but Father held up a hand.

"It's fine, go finish," Father said, standing.

Hunter nodded and went back downstairs, getting dressed in scrubs and gloves again and hoisting Owen onto the table. He stripped him quickly, and it wasn't long before his chest was open.

Hunter removed Owen's heart and placed it in the jar with Alicia's, admiring them both before he screwed the lid on. He then closed Owen's chest cavity and stitched him up.

He had dressed Alicia in a business skirt and shirt and heels, all navy. He dressed Owen in a proper navy suit and smart shoes. He left Owen's hair standing straight up in a mohawk; he found it quirky.

He looked at the clock; there was no time to take them into town now. By the time he got there, people would already be awake and on the street, especially where he was planning to go.

He tossed his scrubs and gloves and went upstairs where Father was reading a book.

"Finished?" Father asked.

Hunter nodded. "I think it's best to move them tomorrow."

"That's fine. The deed was done on their birthday as planned."

Hunter nodded. "I'm going to go to bed. I will wake in the afternoon to get ready to take them."

Father waved him off, and he went upstairs. He stripped naked and climbed into bed, staring up at the ceiling. He sighed, content with his actions, and closed his eyes. He took a few deep breaths before he finally fell asleep.

WHEN HUNTER WOKE, HIS ROOM WAS BRIGHT; HE'D forgotten to close his curtain. He looked at the time; it was almost four. He got up quickly and dressed because he'd slept later than he had intended to. He went downstairs, but there was no sign of Father anywhere. Hunter went out the front door and saw that his truck was gone; he had left.

Hunter went downstairs to check on the bodies of the twins. He inspected his work, and it was perfect—nothing he would do differently.

He went upstairs to make dinner; unsure if Father would be back, he made extra just in case. He could always eat it tomorrow if Father didn't return.

He sat at the table with his bowl of rabbit stew, eating it slowly. He enjoyed every spoon of it, his mind drifting to his next victim already. Martha was going to be easy pickings; he had been following her for a while, and she had predictable movements.

He cleaned his dishes and turned on the radio. He picked up a book and sat down and read, passing the time as best he could. He was excited to get the bodies in place. Once it was late enough, he carried the bodies to his truck and covered them with a tarp before he locked up the cabin and got in, starting the engine.

As he was about to pull off, a set of headlights pulled into the driveway, and then Father pulled his truck next to Hunter's.

"Be careful; don't get caught," Father said once he reached Hunter's window.

Hunter nodded. "There is rabbit stew for dinner."

Father gave a curt nod before he turned and walked toward the cabin. Hunter watched him for a moment before he reversed out of the driveway.

As soon as he hit the service road, he remembered Mike. It was strange that he would think of the chef now, but he remembered him and the pig. He couldn't remember the pig's name. He was glad they were dead. They would have ruined everything.

Hunter gave himself a shake. No point worrying about the dead now. He had work to do. He had to get to Town Hall.

CHAPTER 8

Town Hall, City Center

Danny pulled up to Town Hall. He had gotten the call early; a security guard had found the bodies. Danny showed his badge, donned the necessities, and ducked under the tape, walking to where the tech team was busy taking photos.

"What we got?" he asked.

Tammy, according to her name tag, lowered her camera. "Both shot in the head, like the others."

"We don't know it's the same guy," Danny commented, although he didn't quite believe his own words.

"Willing to bet it is," Tammy said, glancing at him.

Danny snorted. "I wouldn't take the bet with someone else's money."

Richard walked up next to him. "Hey, what we got?"

"A cheeky tech and two dead bodies." Danny grinned at Tammy, who smiled back and resumed taking pictures.

"Same guy?" Richard asked.

"That's what I said," Tammy commented, and Danny rolled his eyes.

"He's never done two bodies before, and what? Does he have two April cubes?"

Richard shrugged. "We'll have to see what Florentine makes of it. This isn't good, though; he's getting more brazen. Mayor is going to be pissed this was done on his doorstep."

Danny sighed. "Don't look now, but you've summoned the devil."

Mayor Bonlow walked down the stairs toward them, his security detail keeping the press behind the crime scene tape. Captain Baker was behind him, looking at the detectives sternly. They were silently being told to behave.

"Gentlemen, why hasn't this been solved yet?" Bonlow asked.

Danny was going to make a crack about having just arrived, but Richard poked him in the side. "Sorry, sir, this one is really slippery."

"I assured the people that we have the best of the best on the case. I do have the best on the case, don't I?" Bonlow raised an eyebrow.

Danny rolled his eyes, and Bonlow narrowed his. "Something to say, Detective?"

"No, sir, just want to get back to it." Danny smiled.

Bonlow eyed him out suspiciously and then stepped in, lowering his voice, "Sort this out, or find yourself new jobs."

He turned and started toward the press to answer questions. Baker shook his head at Danny then followed, knowing the Mayor would call on him to answer questions as well.

Danny turned back to Richard, who was giving him a dirty look. "You just can't control yourself. You know he can make both our lives hell, don't you, Danny?"

"I don't like him; he's a sleazeball with an agenda."

"Then don't vote for him next election, but as he is mayor, he is our boss's boss, so keep your attitude to yourself, partner." Richard shook his head.

Danny felt chastised and frowned. "You wanted to say something too."

"I wanted to punch his lights out," Richard pointed out. "All I'm saying is until we can brag we've caught Stones, there's no way we're going to piss the mayor off and lose our jobs. We both know no one else will solve this."

Danny shrugged, angry that Richard was right. He didn't want to lose the case because he didn't think anyone else was competent enough to solve the case.

They turned back to the bodies. "No ID again. Hopefully, we can identify these two."

"Don't jinx us," Danny commented. "Guys, please get the bodies to the morgue as soon as you can."

Richard's phone rang, and Danny waited for him as he took a few steps away to answer it.

"You're fucking joking," Richard said loudly before looking at Danny wide-eyed. His partner looked back at him curiously.

"We'll be there shortly, yes, thank you." Richard hung up. "It's our lucky day; we might have an ID for John Doe."

Danny hurried to keep up with Richard. "Who was that?"

"Missing persons. Apparently, they were going through some older cases and came across a report about a missing scout master who matches our victim."

"Thank God," Danny proclaimed, heading for his car. "Meet you at the station."

They both drove rather recklessly as they made their way back to the station, weaving in and out of traffic. They reached the station within seconds of each other, with Danny getting there first and taking a prime parking spot.

Richard cursed him as he reached him at the doors. They turned left and took the elevator to the third floor, then approached the front desk.

"Hi, I'm here to see Kevin," Richard explained to the receptionist.

She picked up a phone, "Kevin, there's a...." She looked at Richard.

"Detective Jones," he said quickly.

"There's a Detective Jones here to see you at the front... Okay... Yes, I will... Thank you." She hung up and pointed to the door to her left that was open. "Down the hall, third door on your right."

Richard led Danny through the door, hurrying down the passage past people sitting in chairs looking devastated. Families looking for their loved ones.

Richard knocked on the door and a deep, "Come in" called out.

Richard opened the door, waiting for Danny to walk through, and then shut it. "Kevin?" Richard asked.

"Detective Jones, thanks for coming so quickly." Kevin was a large man, bald with a beard. He shook Richard's hand, then Danny's. He picked up a file, flipped it open to a photo, and handed it to them. "This your victim?"

"Yes!" Danny exclaimed it louder than he intended and blushed slightly. "Sorry, it's just we've been trying to find him for ages. Who is he?"

"Scout Master Timothy Howel. He went missing after he left a camping trip a month ago. He was supposed to take the bus back to the city to meet up with friends for his birthday, but he didn't make it." Kevin put his hands on his hips.

"He didn't make it back to the city?" Danny asked.

"Didn't make it back to the bus apparently," Kevin shrugged. "They thought maybe he got injured or lost in the forest. We've had search teams out weekly combing through the forest for a sign of him, but they didn't find anything."

"The forest again," Danny said to Richard. "And on his birthday. He definitely has a pattern."

Richard looked up at Kevin. "Can I keep this?" He indicated the file. "I'll have it properly transferred to homicide."

"It's all yours, sad to hear he's dead but glad the friends can have some closure now," Kevin said sadly.

Danny nodded, taking the file from Richard. "This is a great help. Thank you so much."

Richard followed Danny out of the office and back toward the elevator. "They're all definitely being murdered in the forest. We can send out a media release to avoid it for now."

"No, he'll just find a new hunting ground; that isn't going to stop this," Danny commented.

"Maybe a new hunting ground will be how we catch him," Richard suggested as the elevator dinged to their floor. They walked toward their desks, putting the picture of Timothy up next to the morgue photo they had up.

Danny shook his head. "No, this guy...this guy knows his stuff; he's not going to be caught easily."

"You said that about Bullseye," Richard said.

"I know," Danny rubbed the stubble on his face. "And I swear the two are connected, Richard, if I can just find—"

"There's no connection, Danny. You need to stop obsessing over Bullseye and focus on the case at hand." Richard threw his hands in the air, frustrated. "We haven't found a connection to him yet, and you're not going to. There are other killers, Danny, other sickos out there. I know you want to catch Jack Waters, but take a step back and help me here first."

Danny watched him with a quirked eyebrow. "Are you done?"

Richard put his hands on his hips angrily. "Yes, I'm done. Are you?"

Danny stared at him, frowning. "Yeah, I'm done." He turned and walked out of the precinct.

"Danny, come back," Richard called.

Danny ignored him and continued on his way out, walking to his car. He had just opened the driver's side door when Richard caught up with him.

"Danny, come on. We have to work, man," he said. "I know what I said upset you, but you have to admit there's truth in my words."

Danny looked at him calmly. "I'll choose to believe what I want to believe, Richard, even if it means I don't share it with you anymore to keep your sanity. Right now, though, I'm going to head to the morgue to see what Florentine has found out about our new victims."

Richard put a hand on his shoulder. "You don't want your partner to come along?"

"Maybe," Danny smiled. "Are you going to lose your shit again like a little girl?"

Richard snorted. "You're a fine one to talk, storming out of the office like a drama queen." He walked to the passenger door and opened it.

"You were definitely the bigger drama queen, Jones," Danny proclaimed, starting the car and getting out of the parking garage and onto the main road.

Danny started looking for parking outside of the morgue.

"We come here so often, we should have reserved parking," Richard muttered.

Danny smiled. "Don't waste the funds on reserved parking. Just pay me overtime."

"Agreed," Richard chuckled.

Once they had parked, they walked. There was no one at the front desk, so they just let themselves into the back and down the corridor. They found Florentine at his desk in the morgue making notes.

"Twins," he said. "Only one cube, but both hearts are missing."

"Can you identify them?" Richard asked. "Or are we going on another wild hunt with these two?"

"No, I managed to identify them through the DMV. Meet Alicia and Owen Medal. Twins from Midtown who were killed approximately two days ago. Want to know what also happened two days ago?" Florentine asked.

"Their birthday?" Richard answered him.

"We have a winner," Florentine gave a macabre smile. "It was their birthday. I also found some dirt in Owen's hair; want to guess where that kind of dirt is most commonly found?"

"The national forest," Danny said quickly. "We need to trace their steps, everyone's steps, and see where and when they are entering the forest and for what reason. We know Donovan went on a hike and Bianca on a date. Timothy went for a camping trip, but these two don't seem like the outdoors type. It doesn't fit."

"How do you know they're not outdoors types?" Richard asked curiously.

"They're soft-looking, they don't have rough hands, and I doubt Florentine found forest dirt on them." Danny looked at the doctor.

"Only Donovan had forest dirt in his wounds," Florentine confirmed. "So it is possible."

"Twenty bucks says they're not outdoors people," Danny said, taking the note out of his wallet and putting it on the cabinet next to Florentine.

Richard took out one as well. "I say they are."

Florentine took out his wallet and put a twenty down. "I say they are too."

Danny smirked. "I love making easy money. Let's go find out more about them to see if they liked the outdoors."

Richard smiled and followed Danny out of the morgue.

IT WASN'T HARD TO TRACE THE TWINS' PARENTS, AND THEY were on their way there when Richard looked at Danny. "How are things going with the family?"

"Why?" Danny asked.

Richard shrugged. "Just wondering."

Danny pursed his lips. "I guess things are going okay. Although with all the long hours I'm working, I'm not really seeing them, so they could literally be on fire, and I probably wouldn't know."

Richard chuckled, "Don't be too hard on yourself, buddy; it's the job. Lexie knew that getting involved with you."

"Did she really, though?" Danny asked, glancing at him as he turned onto the correct street. "She knew it would be hard, but I don't think she realized how hard."

"Speak to her about it," Richard suggested. "You'll see she understands."

Danny snorted and pulled the car to a stop outside a beautiful purple house. There were luminous ornaments in the garden and a pride flag flying high next to an

American flag near the steps that led up to the front door.

The detectives were approaching the front door when a deep voice to their left surprised them. "Can I help you?"

Danny looked at the older gentleman. He was dressed in bright clothes covered in dirt, with gardening tools in his hands. His was covered in tattoos, but his hair was purely gray.

Danny cleared his throat. "Hi, I'm Detective Cox, and this is Detective Jones. We're looking for Mr. and Mrs. Medal?"

"It's Mr. and Mr. Medal," the man said. "But please, to differentiate, call me Jason. My husband Brandon is inside making lemonade."

Richard nodded. "We should probably speak to you both together."

Looking concerned, Jason set his tools down and dusted himself off. "Follow me."

He led them around back where a giant of a man was setting out glasses for lemonade. "Oh, I didn't know we have guests; I'll get more glasses."

"No, it's okay, thank you," Danny held up a hand, "It's really important we speak to you."

Brandon frowned. "What's this about?"

"Can we sit?" Richard asked, indicating the chairs around the table. There were four, two for the parents and two for the children. Danny felt his stomach drop;

he couldn't imagine sitting on the other side of this conversation.

Richard sensed the change in Danny's energy and said, "Are you the parents of twins? Owen and Alicia Medal?"

"What happened to them?" Jason asked, gripping the sides of his chair tightly.

"I'm sorry, sir, but they've been murdered," Richard said apologetically.

Jason looked away, and Brandon swallowed hard. "How?" he gasped out.

"I don't want to know," Jason stood up, "You're wrong. It can't be." He took out his phone. "This is one of their stupid pranks; I'm calling them and telling them this isn't funny."

"Please, Jason, it's not a prank. You heard about the bodies found outside Town Hall?" Danny asked.

"Oh, God." Jason sat back down, shaking uncontrollably.

"Did the twins often visit the forest at all?" Richard asked quietly.

"No, not at all," Brandon said. "They weren't the nature types like us. It was even an effort to get them to keep plants at their places."

Jason was staring off.

"Do you know if they had any enemies or even any new friends?" Danny asked. "I'm sorry we have to ask questions now, but we need as much information as we can get."

"Why? You haven't solved the other murders," Jason snapped at him, glaring at him with pure hatred. Danny sat back, surprised.

Brandon put a hand on Jason's arm. "Love, it doesn't help to bite. Let's see if we can help them."

The detectives gave them a moment to compose themselves before Brandon nodded. "What was the question?"

"Did they have any enemies, or did they maybe make some new friends recently?" Danny asked.

"Not that we know of," Jason's voice was quiet, weak. "They have been hanging around that new restaurant on High Street in Midtown."

"Which restaurant is that?" Richard asked as he took notes.

"Oh, what's it called...Bar...Barfly? No...it's fancier," Jason mused.

"Barthley Dining," Brandon whispered. "They've been eating at Barthley Dining."

Richard nodded and wrote down the name. "We'll check out if there's a connection there, thank you."

"If you think of anything else, please contact us." Danny held out his business card.

Jason reached and took it. "I know you're going to promise me that you're going to catch this guy, but you haven't yet... Just promise me you'll do your best."

"Of course, sir, I always do, and I will catch this guy. He will pay for what he's done." Danny stood up, leading Richard back around the house and to the car.

"Rough times," Richard sighed as they started to drive away.

Danny shook his head. "I couldn't imagine something happening to one of the girls or Lexie. I don't know what I'd do. I'd go crazy."

"I know." Richard gave him a sad smile. "I know you would, Danny, but nothing is going to happen to them."

"You don't know that. We can never be sure. Those two didn't think anything was going to happen to their children."

"Well, we have to hold onto hope, Danny, otherwise you are going to go crazy." Richard looked out of his window. "Do you want to check out this restaurant?"

"You can," Danny sighed. "I'll drop you at the station. I'm going to continue looking at that list Malik gave us, 'cause the answer is definitely on there."

Richard nodded. "Okay, Danny."

Danny pulled into the station and immediately saw the flock of media hanging around. The minute they saw Richard and Danny step out of the car, they flocked to them, demanding answers to impossible questions.

Danny and Richard shouldered their way through the crowd, repeatedly saying, "We don't have any new information at this time," and "We have no comment to make."

Once in the safety of the station, Richard set his notebook down on his desk and said, "I'll check out the restaurant tomorrow maybe. I doubt it'll lead to anything, but I'm not going back out in that now."

"Imagine how I feel," Captain Baker said from behind him. "Because they now follow me around the whole day, no matter what I'm doing."

Danny sat up straight. "We're doing our best to capture him, sir."

"Your best isn't good enough. I'm ready to assign new detectives to this case," Baker said. "Maybe it needs fresh eyes."

Danny stood up angrily. "Are you fucking kidding me?"

Baker took a step toward him. "Watch yourself, Detective. I'm not in the mood to pussyfoot around your feelings today. Hand the case files over to White and Hodges. Take a break; maybe once you calm down, I'll let you assist them on the case."

Danny glared at him, but Richard stepped between them. "I'll get the files to them today," Richard held up his hands. "Danny and I will pick something else to work on."

Baker glared back at Danny before turning around and leaving. Richard whipped around. "You can't speak to your boss that way."

"We've been working our asses off for this case, Richard," Danny growled. "And he's swiping all the hard work to give to other detectives who won't give it the precision and care we will."

"Well then, we'll just have to do something about that," Richard said. "Might mean making an enemy of the captain, though."

Danny raised an eyebrow. "I'm listening."

Richard looked around and leaned forward. "Let's leak it to the news."

"You're mad," Danny said. "Baker will have our balls for breakfast."

"Yeah, but he won't be able to take us off the case." Richard smiled.

Danny thought about it for a moment and then nodded. "I assume you have a more discreet way of doing this than putting *us* on the news."

Richard chuckled. "Leave it to me, buddy."

CHAPTER 9

Hunter understood the concept of a birthday to be the celebration of someone entering the world, but Father said that it was a ridiculous practice, one that they would not observe much like other holidays that Hunter had read about.

Still, Hunter was curious and would have liked to experience a birthday celebration at least once in his life, just for the experience. Father would be so angry if he knew that Hunter thought this way. Father said Hunter was too soft, that he needed to toughen up if he was going to survive in this world.

Hunter thought he'd survive just fine; he understood people better than Father thought. They were sentimental and took things to heart; Hunter didn't do that. He was tough like Father and smart too.

Father would leave him when he had to go pretend to work, to fit in with society, so no one knew who he really was. It was important their family remained a secret. It had for generations.

Hunter had never met his grandfather, but Father spoke of him highly and how high his kill count was before he retired. Hunter wanted to top that kill count. He would be the best and would make Father so proud.

Father would be returning tonight, so Hunter fried some steaks from the freezer after defrosting them. He also made up the plates with tinned corn and instant mash potatoes. To finish it off, he made some gravy and poured on generous amounts. He set the table, turned the radio on, and sat down, sitting on his hands as he waited.

On the hour, he heard the sound of Father's truck's tires driving onto their driveway. Hunter tried to calm himself down. Father didn't like it when he was excited, even if it was to see him.

Father opened the door and walked in, a box in his hands. Hunter turned to look at him curiously—the box was moving excitedly.

Father set it down and took off his coat and hat, hanging them by the door. He looked at Hunter, no trace of a smile. "Hello, Hunter."

"Hello, Father, dinner is ready," Hunter responded.

"Come here first," Father said, kneeling down to the box. Hunter got up and walked slowly over to him.

"It's okay," Father said. "I have a gift for you."

"A gift?" Hunter asked. "Like for a birthday?"

"Yes, just like for a birthday or Christmas." Father eyed him out.

Hunter's brows furrowed. "But you said we don't—"

"Do you not want the gift?" Father asked sternly.

Hunted shook his head. "No, of course, I do. I've never had a gift before."

"Open it." Father stood and put his hands on his hips.

Hunter opened the box and looked inside; confused, he looked up at Father. "It's a puppy? For me?"

"So you're not alone anymore," Father explained.

Hunter reached in and brought the little animal out of the box. The cute, little, furry puppy snuffled and licked Hunter's face excitedly.

"He's a beagle. A decent animal. He'll need a name." Father looked at Hunter.

"I will name him Brother." Hunter looked up at Father for approval.

"Then Brother it is. He is your responsibility. Anything happens, you'll be punished." Father walked to the table and sat down. "Put him back in the box and come eat. You can take him outside to use the toilet after."

Hunter dragged the box over to his place at the table

and set Brother in it. He couldn't help the big smile on his face as he ate his food excitedly.

He'd never had anything alive before; Father said sentimentality was for the weak. Hunter didn't want to question his change of heart because he was so excited to have Brother.

Once he'd taken Brother out to use the toilet, he brought him in and took him upstairs to show him where he'd sleep. Father didn't call him for anything, so they stayed there the remainder of the night, Hunter researching how to train Brother to do tricks and hunt.

As the weeks progressed, Hunter trained Brother to sit, stand, turn around, roll over, and pretend to die. It was so different with Brother in the house; Hunter didn't realize how alone he'd felt when Father left until he had Brother to speak to. The little puppy was growing slowly and loved Hunter with his whole heart, his tail constantly wagging as he followed Hunter around while doing chores.

The days turned to weeks, and weeks turned to months. Brother made an excellent hunting dog the more that Hunter trained him. He was gearing up to show Father what a wonderful decision Brother was by showing him what he could do as a hunting dog.

Father had been gone for two weeks, and Hunter's birthday was approaching, so Hunter decided to cele-brate it with Brother. He had never celebrated a birthday before, and he didn't have much to work with. He used some paper to make some decorations and cut out the shape of balloons to stick up.

He didn't know how to make a cake, so he made pancakes with extra syrup, one of the only dessert dishes he knew how to make. He sat at the table, a stack of pancakes in Brother's bowl sans syrup. Hunter tucked into his pancakes, groaning with pleasure as the warm sugary goodness coated his mouth.

He jumped suddenly when the door opened, Father standing there looking at him. Hunter's eyes went wide, and he stood up quickly, swallowing hard.

"Father, I didn't think you were coming back until—"

"Next week? I thought I'd check in on you," he walked into the cabin, leaving the door open, "What is this?" He gestured to the decorations and pancakes.

"I...I..." Hunter stuttered, not sure what to say.

"You celebrating your birthday, Hunter?" Father asked, looking down at him.

Hunter nodded sadly.

"Well, eat your pancakes," Father said, sitting opposite him. "Then I have something for you."

Hunter sat down nervously and resumed eating his pancakes. He glanced at Brother to see he had already finished and was licking his bowl clean. They sat in silence while Hunter ate.

Once he was done, he washed the dishes and packed them away before going back to Father.

"Come outside," Father said. "Both of you."

Hunter called Brother, and they went outside into the cool night. Hunter was used to the darkness of the night, and with the moon full in the sky, they could see pretty well.

Father stopped at his truck and turned around, nothing in his hands.

Hunted looked up at him curiously. Father unsheathed a knife from his belt and held it out to Hunter. "Take it."

Hunter shakily took the knife and looked at it, then up at Father.

"Now, slit Brother's throat," Father commanded.

Hunter's eyes widened, and his heart felt like it was exploding in his chest. "Father, please don't—"

Father struck him across the face. "Do it now or so help me, I'll slit yours."

Tears formed in Hunter's eyes as he took the knife in his hand and knelt by his dog. Brother looked up at Hunter with such wide loving eyes, his tail wagging excitedly back and forth as Hunter gripped his neck.

"I'm so sorry," Hunter murmured before placing the sharp knife against Brother's throat and slitting it open.

The puppy gave one quick yelp and then made the most heart-wrenching gurgling sound as it started to choke on its own blood. Hunter watched as the light faded from Brother's eyes, and he felt so cold inside.

"Your gift is a lesson about being sentimental. This is

what it gets you." Hunter stood up and tried to stab Father, but Father grabbed his arm mid-air and laughed. "You foolish little child, you got so wrapped up in a puppy that you forget your purpose; best you get to the shed so I can remind you." Father yanked the knife out of Hunter's hand and dragged him toward the shed.

2021 - Present Day

May - Lily

Lily looked out of her apartment window; she had been in a bad space for a few months now. It was almost a year. Yes, a year, a year since her husband of nearly seventy years had passed away.

A year since she had said goodbye to the father of her children, the man who had gone to war for his country twice and who had come back to her each time. She had loved him with every fiber of her being, and she wasn't sure how she would continue without him.

She looked around her apartment, the boxes scattered, open, and half full. She was looking forward to moving to her daughter's house; she would see the grandchildren every day and have company again, but it still wouldn't be the same.

This had been their home since Roy had retired. They had made it their own. She appreciated that her daughter had built her a cottage on her farm so she'd still have privacy, but it would not be the same.

While she was still in the city, she took a bus to the cemetery every day to speak to Roy. She felt comfort standing above his grave, knowing the plot next to him was already reserved for the day she would join him, and they'd be together again.

She looked at the time. She had better get going; she was already running late to get to the cemetery.

She put her coat on, then her broad hat before picking up her purse and heading downstairs. If she wasn't fast enough, she would miss the bus.

She stood at the bus stop, waiting patiently. It was barely a minute before the bus stopped in front of her. She swiped her tag and took her seat in the front. It was quite a distance, but she didn't mind. They left the city center, and she had to change buses, then it was another fifteen minutes before she stepped off the bus.

She walked in silence as a fine drizzle started to rain down on her. She hadn't brought an umbrella with her, but it wasn't a hard rain, and it wouldn't hurt her. She just tugged her coat closer around her. She walked into the cemetery and up the pathway. She knew the way well.

She stood in front of Roy's grave, looking at the headstone sadly. She told him about the packing and how their daughter Zelia would get her a cat, which she was excited about. She said she knew he had hated cats, but it would be something to keep her busy while everyone was out of the house during the day.

She stood there for a long time, simply talking. She didn't even hear anyone approaching until he was right next to her. She clutched her chest and gasped.

"You scared me, young man." She eyed the young police officer.

"Sorry, ma'am," Hunter said; he had a rough voice, as though he wasn't used to using it. "I saw you standing in the rain and wanted to offer you a ride back to the city."

"Yes, please, that would be wonderful," Lily kissed her fingers and touched Roy's grave before taking Hunter's extended arm and letting him lead her to his car. It wasn't a police car, but that didn't cause her any alarm.

He helped her in and got in on the driver's side. He started the car, and they pulled off onto the road.

"Allow me to take you on a nice scenic route back," he offered. "I'm sure you'll enjoy the sight of the forest."

"I don't want to be a bother." But Lily smiled as though she would be grateful for the company.

"Not at all. I'm off duty now, so it's no trouble at all," Hunter said.

"That's so sweet of you, thank you, dear. What's your name?" Lily asked curiously.

"Hunter," he said honestly. "My name is Hunter."

"It's a pleasure to meet you, Hunter. So nice to meet someone whose parents brought him up right." Lily nodded as though she was an expert on this topic.

As they neared the entrance to the forest, Hunter reached down his side and pulled out a gun, aiming at Lily's head. She was looking out of the window and hadn't noticed the movement. Before she could turn, Hunter pulled the trigger, and blood splattered against the window.

He put the gun away and turned onto the service road. He navigated his way through the forest.

That was five. He only needed seven more to complete his collection. Then Father would retire and give Hunter his freedom to continue as he pleased. This was his final assignment, and he would have one hell of a graduation party when it was done, starting with those nosy detectives.

Once he reached the cabin, he carried Lily's fragile frame from his stolen car to the basement. He would dispose of the vehicle later. The police hadn't found the cab he'd disposed of yet; they wouldn't find this one either.

He undressed Lily and replaced her heart with the May cube. He applied some makeup to her face and dressed her up in an outfit worthy of the queen—something Father had arranged while away on one of his trips. It was perfect.

He carried her body back upstairs, stopping as Father came inside the cabin. Father looked at Lily and nodded. "Don't get caught, and don't be seen."

"Yes, Father," Hunter said, walking out through the

door and putting Lily on the back of his truck, and covering her with a tarp. He retrieved her purse, taking out most of the contents except her ID. He wanted to show everyone that he wasn't afraid of being caught, that he couldn't be caught.

He pulled out and made his way back to the service road. He was pleased with himself, and he knew who was next. And the next victim after that, and the one after that. It had all been worth it for the year of preparation. Some victims had to be changed because they'd moved or circumstances changed, but most were pretty predictable.

June, in his opinion, was a mercy killing anyway. He turned on his radio to a classical station, humming softly as he drove and thought about his next task.

CHAPTER 10

WALTAR'S MALL, CITY OUTSKIRTS

Danny bit into his hotdog as he watched Kira step up to pitch for her girls' baseball team. Lexie was screaming for her daughter as she bounced up and down next to him. It was a beautiful Saturday to be out in the sun. Danny was trying to focus on the game, trying not to go over the Stones case in his mind while he watched. He needed to be more present in his family's life, or he would lose them.

He swallowed his bite and cheered as the first pitch was a strike. He smiled and looked to his left at Cleo, who was on her phone, and Thea, who was reading a book.

"Come on, guys, Kira's up," Danny said. "Pay attention."

Both Cleo and Thea scoffed, and Danny rolled his eyes, smiling at Lexie. He stuffed the last bite of his hotdog in his mouth and wiped his hand before putting an arm around her shoulders. Lexie clapped her hands, cheering Kira on. It was another strike. Their section erupted in cheers.

"One more, pitcher," someone shouted.

"Come on, Kira," one of the other mothers screamed excitedly.

Danny's phone rang, and he groaned, taking it out of his pocket and glancing at it.

Lexie frowned. "Danny, she's pitching. Just give it a moment."

"It's dispatch. I have to take it," he mumbled, answering the call. He used his finger to block his other ear so he could hear.

The stands erupted in cheers as Kira threw another strike, and the batter was out. Danny knelt. "Yeah? Okay. Yes. Text me the address."

When he stood up, he saw Kira looking right at him, and he smiled, giving her a thumbs up.

Kira shook her head and turned away from him, and Danny sighed. "Doghouse again for me tonight."

"What's new?" Cleo snorted.

"Let us guess, Dad, you gotta bounce. Some big crime scene?" Thea didn't even glance up.

"Yeah, yeah, you guys will understand one day," he

promised, kissing Lexie gently. "Sorry, honey, it's a new victim, the same guy."

"Be safe," Lexie said with a sad smile.

Danny kissed both his daughters' heads. "Be good, girls."

He shuffled through the stands and made his way to the bottom; as he reached the ground, he caught Kira's eye and gave her a sad wave. She returned his wave and went back to her game.

Danny called Richard. "Where are you?"

"I know you're with your family at the game, so I'm on my way to get you. Head to the parking lot," he said.

"Thanks." Danny hung up and went to the parking lot.

He didn't have to wait long before he saw Richard's car. He made his way over and climbed in.

"What have we got?" Danny asked.

"I know about as much as you do, a victim shot in the head posed at the mall," Richard recited.

"A mall, though? How'd he get in? There must be cameras?" Danny sighed. "Can we stop at my house so I can change and grab my badge and gun?"

"Sure," Richard said, turning right.

"Hopefully, we can get this guy this time." Danny sighed, sitting back and taking off his baseball cap.

Once he had changed and donned his badge and gun, he returned to the car, climbing in and nodding. "Let's go."

The mall was abuzz with media. They saw Baker there, who had been riding their asses since the media mysteriously got tipped off that Baker was changing detectives. The public had not responded kindly. Baker couldn't prove it was them, though, so there was no disciplinary action, but Danny knew if they didn't get this guy, it would cost them their jobs.

They avoided the media and ducked under the tape to get their gloves and booties before approaching the scene. Danny sat on his haunches and looked up at her.

"This must be his oldest victim yet," Danny muttered.

Baker walked over. "We have some good news, though."

Danny stood up, next to Richard, and looked at his boss expectantly. "Cameras?"

"No, they were disabled. But tech says her ID was in her bag, along with a few other things," Baker explained. "This might be the break we need."

Danny nodded. "Who is she?"

"Lily Clarke, city resident and pensioner. Her address was in a small diary in the purse. We're going to go inspect her apartment and contact next of kin."

"Don't we normally do that?" Richard asked, cocking his eyebrow.

"Oh, since I can't throw you off this case, I'm going to give you two new directions on how to handle it. I'm having all things related to locations from all victims' apartments or homes brought to the station, and you're going to go through it and establish a connection."

"That could take ages," Danny frowned. "Who's going to go to the morgue or track leads?"

"I'm pulling other detectives onto the case to...assist you," Baker smirked, "They can do some chasing since you're the ones who know the victims so well and are the better choice to go through the evidence."

Richard glared at Baker. "No case is clean-cut, and you want to play politics with this one?"

"I know you two leaked information to the media," Baker growled. "I can't prove it, but I know it, and you'll be lucky to get out from behind your desk before you retire." He turned and stormed off.

Danny ran a hand over his head. "Great, this is just what we need."

"We'll work around it," Richard assured him.

Danny shook his head. "Why is he fighting us on this so much?"

"Don't get into politics, Danny. We aren't built for them," Richard advised, turning back to the body. "Who knows, maybe we will break the case that way."

Danny turned and looked past the body, searching the surrounding area. He stopped and cocked his head. "You didn't find anything at that fancy restaurant, did you?"

"Barthleys? No, I didn't," Richard looked at him, "Why?"

"Something's bugging me, but I can't place my finger on it," Danny murmured.

Richard patted his shoulder. "It'll come to you, come on, let's get to the station and start sorting shit."

They walked away from the crime scene, disposing of their gloves and booties. They shouldered their way through the media and back to the car.

As they drove, Danny stared out of the window, his mind racing with thoughts but at the same time devoid. It was as though something was dangling just out of his grasp, and he shook his head.

"Richard, humor me," Danny said.

"Okay..."

"Just humor me; what if Bullseye isn't the killer, but he's involved some way?" Danny didn't look at him. "What if he's working with someone else?"

"A dynamic killing duo? I love it," Richard said sarcastically. "Maybe they're going to start a league of extraordinary villains."

Danny frowned and glared at him. "Hey, I asked you to humor me."

"Not when it comes to Bullseye, Danny; you're obsessed with him. You need to set him aside until we're done with this case." Richard pulled into the parking lot and found a spot.

They got out, and Danny slammed his door. "It'll take a while for the stuff to arrive; I'm going for a drink." He stormed off.

He heard Richard call him, but he ignored him and left the parking lot, heading down the road to the bar.

He ordered a beer and sat there mulling over it. He was halfway through when the seat next to him was pulled out, and Jerome sat down.

"Hey, Danny." He signaled the barman for a beer.

"Aren't you retired? You should be golfing or something." Danny sipped his beer.

"Not allowed to visit the old watering hole still?" Jerome asked, chuckling. "I'm actually here to speak to you."

Danny frowned. "About what?"

"About Bullseye," Jerome said calmly, taking his beer and sipping it.

"Richard seriously called you in to speak to me; this is fucking bullshit." Danny downed his beer and started to stand.

Jerome put a hand on his arm. "Just hear me out; it's about Bullseye, but it's not."

Danny sat back down, and Jerome ordered him another beer.

"See, I told you I had that case, that one from a few years ago. That case plagued me throughout my career. I obsessed about it much like you're obsessing about Jack

Waters, Danny." Jerome sighed. "I'm saying, I understand. The problem is, I started to link every kidnapped kid case to that one case, and a lot of times, it almost cost the missing kids their lives."

Danny sighed and sipped his beer silently, knowing he couldn't leave until Jerome had his say.

"I'll never forget April 2004 in Newlands. Little Aiden was taken from his parents' garden while his mom went in to get him juice. We canvassed everywhere, but it was as though he had disappeared without a trace."

"Newlands 2004?" Danny asked, setting his beer down.

"Yeah, why?" Jerome asked.

"Jack Waters was a patrolman in that area during that time," Danny commented. "I know 'cause I've traced his every career move."

Jerome looked thoughtful, then he looked away. "No..." he muttered.

"What?" Danny asked.

"I can't be sure, but Jack Waters...I think I remember seeing him at the scene...I can't be sure, mind you, this was years ago."

Danny stood up, knocking his stool over. "Jerome, you fucking genius. I have to go."

Danny strode out of the bar and down the street toward the station. He went straight to his desk and started pulling out files. He inspected them carefully, comparing notes.

Richard came in from the break room and looked at what Danny was looking at. "Oh seriously, Danny—"

"I found the connection, you twit," Danny growled, slamming the files down, pointing to dates. "Jack Waters was a patrolman in Newlands when this kid Aiden went missing."

"So?" Richard asked.

"I think he took the kid. He applied for a sabbatical shortly after that case. He stated mental health as the reason. He didn't return for three years, Richard. I'm telling you, he took this kid."

"Okay, and then?" Richard asked, frustrated.

"Then... Then..." Danny paced and then clicked his fingers. "What if he raised a killer?"

"What?" Richard shook his head. "Danny, you're losing your mind."

"The prisoners we caught back from the bus, they said there was a young guy out to free Jack, right? What if it's his prodigy?"

Richard stared at him for a moment, and Danny was ready to be told he was crazy again when Richard shook his head. "I can't believe it...it actually makes sense."

Danny grinned. "Thank you fucking God, at long last, you're with me."

Richard came over to where the files were splayed

out on Danny's desk. "So we're saying that Jack has a kid?"

"One that he's spent seventeen years training to be a killer," Danny proclaimed. "Think about it, Richard. He has a different MO but skills to evade us like Jack. People don't just wake up and become brilliant serial killers. Most serial killers are a spur-of-the-moment thing. They make a mistake, and they're caught. This is way more Jack Waters' style."

Richard rubbed his stubble. "Okay, I'm going to give you the benefit of the doubt and say I'm with you on this, Danny. How the hell do we track these two down? It was a mission to capture Waters in the first place. Never mind that you've spent a year trying to track him down with no success."

"The clue is in these victims; we need to figure out how he is selecting them, then we can catch them," Danny declared.

Baker cleared his throat from behind them. "This is a really tall order, Detective."

Danny looked at him. "I'm sure of it, sir. Look, I know you're pissed with us, but I'm telling you, this is how we are going to close this case."

"What do you suggest?" Baker asked, sighing.

"That we do what you suggested, go through the victims' things and find a location or anything that ties them together. Once we do that, we can figure out how they're being selected. Hopefully, predict the next victim, and stop them from being killed." Danny made it sound so easy.

Richard nodded. "I'll start going through the stuff."

"Out of that list Malik gave me, three sets of cubes are not accounted for. Two of the people were out of state when we called on them, and one was donated to a charity that auctioned it off to someone named James Jones, who we cannot track anywhere. The address given was fake."

Baker nodded. "So let's see if any of the victims' locations tie in with that charity."

Baker summoned some detectives from their desks. "Come and assist Jones and Cox; this takes priority. They will tell you what they need."

It took them a while to get everyone up to date, but once they were, they moved to the boardroom where all the victims' address books and business cards had been deposited, one box at a time. They each took a box and started to go through it, using the whiteboards to write what they found.

Richard and Danny took turns making coffee for everyone. Danny was going through Bianca's business card holder, which was much thicker than anyone else's. He paused as he turned the page to the 'B' section. He frowned and glanced up at the whiteboards. He scanned them one at a time.

"Barthleys," he murmured. "Hey, everyone, look for something that might tie the victims to Barthleys."

Everyone scrambled and started scanning through what they had, most coming up with a loyalty card or a business card.

Danny stuck them to each relevant board and looked around. "They all went to Barthleys..."

"Yeah, but it's not like we can go to Barthleys and ask them for who dined with them for the last six months; that's insane."

"No..." Danny nodded. "You're right. But maybe... maybe Barthleys sponsors charities." He looked at Richard meaningfully.

Richard's eyes widened. "So the killer may have entered there, what then?"

"What if all our victims did as well?" Danny asked excitedly. "What if that's how he's choosing them?"

"We need to get there," Richard said, grabbing his jacket.

Danny looked around the room. "Keep going through everything in case we're wrong; we'll call you from the location."

They rushed out to Richard's car and put the siren on, zooming through traffic to Barthleys' front door. They stopped just beforehand to take a breath.

"Danny, this could be nothing," Richard reminded him, "It's just a hunch."

"My last hunch cornered Jack Waters," Danny stated. "I know this is it, Richard."

"You are an amazing cop," Richard smiled. "Let's go."

They walked in and immediately asked the hostess to speak to the owner. He wasn't there, so they asked for the head manager in charge.

A tall, older-looking man came to them. "Hi, Detectives, my name is Thomas, and I'm the manager. How can I help you?"

"Is there an office we can talk in?" Richard asked.

"Follow me," he said, straightening his suit and leading them to the back of the restaurant. He indicated they could sit, and he sat behind a large desk.

"Does this restaurant sponsor or host a lot of charity competitions?" Danny asked, taking out his notes.

The manager nodded. "We have one every month; we try to vary them."

"I need to know if you ever had one from a charity called Moonlight Pets, a pet rescue. They were giving away a box with birthstones in it, all in cubes." Richard held his breath.

The manager turned to his computer. "Give me a moment." He typed furiously and scrolled, taking a few moments. "Uh, yes, about two years ago, we hosted that competition. The entrants had to sign up for a newsletter and donate fifty dollars. The winner was a James Jones."

Danny looked at Richard, and he felt a weight

leaving his shoulders. "Thomas, what information did the entrants have to give to sign up for the newsletter?"

"Their name, surname, date of birth, and address," he explained. "Name and surname obviously, and the address was where they wanted the prize delivered. The date of birth was so that the rescue could send special birthday wishes on their special day. I've actually done a few charities with this rescue; they're very good."

Richard asked quietly, "Thomas, what are the chances you have a copy of the entrant list for that competition?"

"Oh, we used an electronic device to capture the information, so I can probably just generate a list for you." Thomas smiled. "Let me do that."

They thanked Thomas as they took the list and returned to the car. Danny scanned through the list quickly. "Donovan is on this list...so is Bianca..." Danny flipped through the pages. "I see Timothy..."

Richard hooted and said loudly, "We're going to catch the dickhead."

"Don't get too excited. We still need to figure out the next victim," Danny said breathlessly.

"Who has a birthday in June?" Richard asked.

Danny started counting through the list. "About twenty people have birthdays in June. We're going to have to narrow this down."

Richard pulled into the station's parking lot and

switched the car off. "But we got him, Danny. We will get him. We are inches away from him."

Danny looked up at him. "I told you."

"You told me," Richard smiled softly. "I'm sorry, Danny, I should have believed you."

"It's okay. When this is over, you can take me out for a decent whiskey, and we'll call it even." Danny smiled back and got out of the car.

They walked confidently back to the police station, victim list in hand.

CHAPTER 11

2006 - 7 YEARS OLD

WHEN HUNTER WOKE UP, IT WAS WARM; HE REALIZED HE MUST have overslept. He got up quickly and went to the bathroom to relieve himself and wash up. Once done, he got dressed and went downstairs. Father had just walked in from outside with their scarecrow under his arm.

"Take a chair and go sit by the tomato plants," Father ordered him. "Don't let one bird near them until I finish fixing this scarecrow."

Hunter wanted to point out he hadn't had breakfast, but he knew how easily Father got upset. Sometimes he threatened to take Hunter to the shed, and Hunter was terrified of what that could mean.

He took a chair and carried it outside and around the

cabin to their little garden. He set the chair down next to the tomato plants and sat on it, watching the plants carefully.

The minutes ticking by felt like hours to Hunter; he wished Father would finish fixing the scarecrow. Doing chores was better than doing this. He wanted to go hunt rabbits or baby deer in the forest and swim in the river to cool down. The hot sun beating down on him didn't help at all.

He didn't know how long he'd been sitting there for, but the sweat was dripping down his face. He wanted to get up and check how far Father was, but again, he was too scared.

He looked around, bored out of his mind. He hummed a little, but other than that, nothing was happening. He hadn't had to get up once to chase away a bird. It was a pointless exercise.

He saw movement in the distance, some bushes rustled, and he sat up, his eyes squinting in the sunlight to see what was there. He looked around and saw a small shovel; he could definitely use it to kill a rabbit and then bring it back for dinner. Father would be so pleased with him.

He took the shovel and quietly made his way out of the garden toward the rabbits. They sat up, eying him out wearily, their ears straight and upright. They took off suddenly into the trees, and Hunter ran after them, dead set to get one. He slowed down and waited for them to as well. He crept forward, not wanting to startle them again. He wished Father would show him how to catch rabbits; he would catch them all the time for dinner.

The rabbits took off again but were only a few paces ahead. Hunter moved after them. It was cooler in the forest, with the trees blocking out the light. He looked around and realized that the sun was already dipping. His eyes widened, and he abandoned the rabbits, knowing Father would be very angry if he found Hunter had left. Hunter sprinted through the woods, his breath coming quickly as he moved his little legs as fast as he could.

He reached the edge of the woods and looked around; there was no one about, so he ran to sit on the chair, throwing down the shovel. He tried to catch his breath, breathing as deeply as he could.

"Something wrong?" Father asked from behind him, making him jump. "Did you not get the rabbits?"

Hunter looked at him, his lip pouting. "I'm sorry, Father, I thought I could catch one for you."

"What did I ask you to do?"

"To guard the tomatoes." Hunter's eyes trailed to the plants; some of the plump fruits were clearly picked at, the birds had had their fill. Father grabbed him by the neck and picked him up.

"If you can't protect our food, then you can't eat it."

"But, Father, I haven't eaten all day," Hunter wailed.

Father dragged him back to the cabin and to an empty closet by the basement stairs. He threw Hunter into the closet. "You're lucky I allow you into a closet with a light and a window for fresh air. Once you've paid for your disrespect, you can come out."

Hunter started to bawl, rushing to get up to the door. Father slammed it shut and locked it. Hunter banged against the door, begging for Father to come back for him. He sank to the floor eventually, his tummy aching from the sobbing. He hugged his knees and cried into them as the sun set outside.

He must have eventually fallen asleep because when he woke, the sun was peaking once again. He stood up and opened the tiny window for some fresh air. It was cold, and it stung his cheeks, but it made him feel like he was outside. Like he was free.

He understood why Father was punishing him, he understood he had failed at his task, but he wished Father would at least give him something dry to eat even if it wasn't tasty like rabbit stew.

He waited by the door all day, occasionally getting up to pace in a circle in the small area. When he sat, his leg bounced, and he fidgeted with everything he could touch—his fingers, shirt, pants, and shoelaces.

He couldn't sit still, he was restless, and he was starving. His stomach cramped from wanting food. He couldn't remember what the last thing he ate was, but he would eat anything now, even the sour berries he disliked that Father made him pick and eat. He felt his pants get wet as he couldn't hold his bladder anymore. He whimpered. He knew what would come next.

The sun set again, and he curled up, crying quietly. Exhaustion eventually took over when the night was long dark already, and he slept until the sun streamed through the next morning.

He was shivering because he'd forgotten to close the window at night. He sat up and rubbed his hands and legs as best he could, trying to warm up. He didn't want to close the window because once the sun was up, it would get warm quickly, and hard to cool the closet down.

He stood and banged on the door, tears streaming down his face. "Father, please, I respect you. I do. Please, I'm sorry."

Father didn't come during the day or night.

On the third day, he cried and banged on the door harder, begging to be let out. To his surprise, the door did swing open.

"Are you some small baby that you have shit yourself, pissed yourself...cried all this time?" Father demanded to know. "Go get cleaned up, and come down immediately," Father instructed him.

Hunter left the closet quickly and did as he was told. He had a shower and dressed in clean clothes, setting his dirty clothes aside to be washed. He went downstairs, sniffing.

"You're still sulking," Father growled. "That's it. It's time you met the shed."

Hunter shook his head and backed up. "Father, no, please, I'm sorry."

"This is for your own good, Hunter. You need to become a man; you need to be taught a lesson." Father grabbed his arm painfully and dragged him out of the cabin. Once they were inside the shed, Hunter looked around, trying to see what torture Father had for him.

"Take these steps and set them by the center pole," Father said.

Hunter took them and did as he was told.

"There are two leather hooks at the top of the pole. You need to climb the steps, climb the pole, and loop your hands through them." Hunter started to climb the steps, but Father put a hand on his shoulder. "First, you strip naked, boy."

Hunter looked at him in surprise, but not wanting to incur more wrath, he stripped naked and did as he was told. Once he was hanging, he heard Father behind him.

"I've been too soft on you, boy; you're going to learn quickly what it takes to be part of this legacy," Father said. "If you let go, you will climb back up there and receive more, you understand?"

"More what?" Hunter asked fearfully.

Suddenly a searing pain spread through his back as something leather struck him. He gasped out a sob and nearly let go.

"I wouldn't if I were you." But it was too much. Hunter dropped down, narrowly missing the floor.

"Up again," Father ordered.

Hunter whimpered and got up, climbing up the stairs, climbing the pole, and looping his hands in. He bit his lip hard as he was struck again and again.

He lost count of how many times Father hit him before he stepped away, leaving Hunter to hang there for a few minutes before he said, "You can come down now. Get dressed and go eat. I made a rabbit stew yesterday, and there is some left over; you can heat it up."

Hunter winced as his muscles screamed from his movement. He slid down the pole to the steps, nearly tumbling off. He got dressed gingerly and as he was about to pass Father, Father grabbed his face and lifted it to look at him. "This will only happen when you disobey me or fail at a task. Do you understand?"

Hunter nodded, and Father's fingers dug into his face painfully.

"Say it out loud."

"Yes, Father, I understand," he said, trying to be clear when he was terrified.

Father let him go, and Hunter hurried to the house. Too scared to look back at the shed in case he was dragged back there.

2021 - Present Day

June - William

It had been a long journey. He had enjoyed a prosperous life. He had been known for his tenacity and success, but where were his worldly possessions now? Thirty-nine and dying of cancer. He could afford the chemo-therapies, but nothing had stopped it from spreading like wildfire through his failing body. He felt too young to be taken from this world.

He had found love, but he had pushed her away once he was diagnosed; she didn't need to waste her time looking after someone no better than an infirmed old man. He wouldn't have her changing his diapers or spoon-feeding him. He wouldn't have anyone doing that.

God help him; he would go out of this world on his own terms if he could help it. That's why he hadn't gone to his last few treatments.

He could almost feel the cancer in his bones, and now without the chemo holding it back, it was growing worse, but he needed the strength he had to do this his way.

Chemo wiped him out, and he didn't want to die lying in a hospital bed, considered some sort of vegetable by medical students. He wasn't even fit to donate his organs to someone to continue their life. He was rendered worthless.

They had sent him to counseling, but it had pretty much been sessions to get him ready for his death.

However, they didn't say anything about him having to wait for the cancer to take him before he died.

No.

He was leaving this Earth his way.

He drove out toward the national forest; he knew a great place to do it. Somewhere remote where no one could stop him. He had been on a dark web forum talking to other terminally ill and depressed people who wanted to take their own lives.

He had told them his plan, that he would go to his local national forest on his birthday and end it all. He thanked them for understanding; at least they knew what it was like. Everyone else may call him a coward or pity him, but they understood how brave this was.

He parked his car and sat there a moment. He pulled the gun out of his glove compartment and hid it in his jacket. He looked at his will, left on the passenger seat of his car. He climbed out and left the keys inside of it. He wouldn't need them anymore.

He walked toward the hiking trails, but just before reaching them, he veered off to a side path, making his way into the trees. He wanted to be deep in the woods when he did this, as far as he could make it.

It was cool in the shade, and once he was out of sight, he pulled his hand holding the gun out, and let it hang by his side. The weapon felt so heavy his arm ached from carrying the weight. He had to judge this carefully. He couldn't go too far, or he wouldn't have the energy to complete his task, but he didn't want to come up short so that someone might stumble upon him and stop him.

He came to a clearing and saw a man sitting there. He quickly hid the gun in his jacket, trying not to groan from the sudden movement. The man simply sat there, polishing his gun.

"Sorry, didn't mean to disturb you," William mumbled. "I'll be on my way."

"I can help you with what you want," it was a deep, rough voice, and William raised an eyebrow.

"What's that?"

"Ending it," Hunter looked up at him. "I don't mind pulling the trigger."

William looked deep into his eyes and realized this man was definitely a killer. He suddenly felt a little nervous about his plan; he had wanted to go out on his own terms. He didn't want to be murdered. Who knew what the guy would do to his body?

"I don't know what you're talking about," William stammered.

"Pity," Hunter stood up, raising his gun, "I thought you'd be the easiest one."

CHAPTER 12

Danny stretched; they'd been at the station for three straight nights, going home only to shower.

"Richard, we have another June. This guy, William Kitchener, he's a successful businessman that signed up for the competition. His birthday is today."

"Today?" Richard said. "How the hell are we going to find him on such short notice?"

Danny shook his head. "We need to find him somehow. I've got his address; we can start at his house."

Richard sighed. "Is he the only one for today?"

They'd been chasing people every day of June that had a birthday that was on the list, trying to make sure they weren't the victim. They were exhausted. Now, after three days at the station trying to narrow the list, Richard felt like he was at his wit's end.

Danny looked at him. "Okay, you go and get some sleep. I'll take a look at his house; it's on my way home."

"Thank God," Richard breathed, picking up his jacket. They walked toward their cars together, Danny yawning loudly. "We're close; I can feel it."

"Yeah, we've been saying that all of June," Richard mumbled, stopping at his car. "Go straight home after you find this guy, Danny; you can't think straight if you don't sleep."

"Yeah, yeah, yeah," Danny said, waving him off as he stifled another yawn. Danny punched the address into his GPS and started to drive. It was a little out of the way, he had lied a bit, but it was the only one they had to check today. The guy was probably at home or work, enjoying a relaxing day. Danny envied civilians so much, but he knew his job made a difference.

He parked outside of the house, noting that the driveway was empty. He decided to check the house anyway.

He walked up to the door and knocked hard; before he could do anything, the door swung open, unlocked. Danny frowned, drawing his gun. "Mr. Kitchener?" he called. "It's Detective Cox from the police department; this is just a courtesy check."

He walked in slowly, holding his gun, ready to fire. He checked each room as he went, but everything seemed fine. He saw a note on the computer and went to read it. It said, **I'M NOT SORRY**.

Danny frowned as he took out a surgical glove, put it on, and picked up the note. As he did, he bumped the mouse, and the screen for the computer came to life. Danny looked at it. It was a forum; he scanned the screen and realized it was a really dark one. Looking around, he took the mouse and scrolled up through the posts. This William guy had cancer and was planning on taking his life on his birthday.

Danny cursed and quickly searched for any information on how. He caught the post by William stating he'd go to the local forest. Danny stood straight, dropping the letter to the table. He quickly calculated the closest entrance and decided Donovan liked to hike there. He rushed out of the house, leaving the door open.

He climbed into his car, not wanting to put on a siren, so he didn't scare William. Even if he wasn't the victim, Danny had to help him. He called in a possible suicide attempt on the radio to dispatch and asked them to send emergency services out immediately to the forest. He was closer though; he'd beat them there.

Danny speed-dialed Richard while he drove, putting him on speaker.

"I just got out of the shower, Danny. Come on," he groaned.

"This guy, this possible vic, he's about to try to take his own life in the forest," Danny was urgent. "In the forest where most of the victims have been killed. I need to try to stop him, at least, but he was posting about it on the Internet. What if the killer has been tracking the victims for two years? Tracking them by following them on social media or the Internet. If I'm right, Richard, he knows that Kitchener is going to the forest today."

"Fuck, which entrance? I'll be there soon." Danny could hear Richard getting dressed.

"Near where Donovan hiked," Danny said, drawing a momentary blank.

"Got it, see you soon." Richard hung up, and Danny concentrated on driving, weaving through traffic as best he could without his sirens on. He left the city limits and put his foot down, speeding for the entrance to the forest as best he could. The sun was lowering in the sky. Twilight was upon them. He pulled into the parking lot; most of the people were leaving. Some had dogs while others were buckling in children. Danny looked around, trying to figure out if any of the cars could belong to William.

"Dispatch," Danny radioed in. "Do you have the victim's license plate number?"

"Dispatch to Detective Cox, please hold for license plate number." There was static, and then the dispatch officer read the license plate number to him.

He quickly memorized it and started going from car to car. He'd gone through two rows; when on the third, he found the car. He felt the engine; it was still warm, which meant he couldn't have gone far. Danny opened the car on the passenger side and picked up some papers. It was a will and testament.

Danny cursed and threw them back down. He looked around and saw the entrance to the hiking trails; he quickly made his way toward them, bumping a few people along the way. He had to find Kitchener before Stones did. He couldn't have a sixth victim.

Danny looked up at the various hiking trails; he had only one shot picking the correct one. He thought about it; a cancer patient wouldn't have as much energy to hike. Danny glanced to the side of the trail to a path leading into the woods. Danny radioed in to dispatch about the way he was taking and asked them to let Richard know to join him there.

He then took off down the path, drawing his gun and keeping an eye out in as many directions as he could turn his head in. The forest was cold, like a tomb, and eerily quiet.

Danny looked for any sign that Kitchener had come through this way, but there was none, just the path winding ahead of him. Danny kept his ears peeled.

A shot rang out, and Danny looked straight ahead; he held his gun tightly as he sprinted down the path, panting hard as he moved, sweat dripping down his face from the exertion. He ran into a clearing just as a tall, young-looking man was carrying the body of William Kitchener to the end of the other side.

"Put the body down, and put your hands up," Danny yelled, pointing his gun at Hunter.

Hunter paused and turned around slowly, frowning. "You're playing with fire, Detective, coming out here alone with no backup."

"I wouldn't worry about that if I were you. Drop your gun and put the body down," Danny demanded, keeping his gun trained on Hunter. "Do it now, Aiden."

"Aiden?" Hunter asked curiously. "What makes you think that is my name?"

"Oh, did he change it then?" Danny asked. "After he took you."

"Took me?" Hunter snorted. "What cockeyed theory have the police come up with this time?"

"You were kidnapped from your parents' yard when you were three; your name was Aiden. Your parents are still looking for you. Your mother and father," Danny said, standing still. "Jack Waters took you from your family to raise you to be a killer."

"Father is my only parent," Hunter said calmly. "I don't know what you're talking about."

"You're not stupid. You know how children are made. Where is your mother? Has he ever told you?"

Hunter paused, and Danny saw an opportunity in this.

"What does he call you?"

Hunter stared at him, then said quietly, "Hunter, my name is Hunter."

"Hunter, what?" Danny asked.

Hunter looked at him as though he'd never thought of that.

"Ironic that he named you as the thing he wanted you to be, a hunter, but this isn't your fault. Aiden, you are not the bad guy. You were conditioned to do this, and we can get you help, reunite you with your real family."

"My name isn't Aiden," Hunter said, getting angry. "I have Father, and I am called Hunter. It's my name."

Danny let one hand off his gun and held it up. "It's okay. I know this is a lot to take in. I can't even begin to imagine what he must have put you through."

A branch snapping behind Danny had Hunter dropping Kitchener's body and raising his gun. Danny didn't dare look behind him, but he heard Richard's voice.

"It's true, Aiden, you were a great kid destined to do amazing things. This, this is not who you were meant to be." Richard stepped into Danny's peripheral vision. "Your parents miss you so much."

Hunter shook his head and held the gun steady. "You're lying. Cops lie all the time to get what they want."

Danny shook his head. "No, that's just what Waters wants you to believe because he was a cop that lied."

"He wasn't a cop," Hunter frowned. "He was undercover. He never belonged to your stupid station."

Danny glanced at Richard, who had his gun up and

ready. Danny knew that in no time, the forest would be overrun with cops, and they needed to have Hunter in custody by then. Danny lowered his gun slowly, putting it in its holster.

Hunter glared at him. "What are you doing?"

"I'm showing you that I don't want to hurt you. Aiden, your parents' names are Delilah and Clive. They were young when they had you, but they loved you so much. They still stay in the same house, hoping you'll come back." Danny took a tentative step forward.

Hunter looked at Richard, then Danny. "No, that's not possible."

"You must remember something," Danny said gently. "He took you when you were three; you had three years with your real parents."

"How was he able to take me if they loved me so much?" Hunter spat.

Danny shook his head. "Your mom turned her back for a minute to get you a juice box, and then you were gone. Aiden, come home. We will make a deal with the district attorney to get you treatment rather than put you in prison. You have a strong case. You don't even have to tell me where Jack Waters is. I just want to take care of you."

Hunter dropped his gun slowly. "You don't want to know where Father is?"

"I want to know," Danny nodded. "But I will find him one way or another. It doesn't have to involve you.

Right now, I'm worried about you and getting you the help you need."

Hunter stared at him. "You want to get me help? I don't need help. There is nothing wrong with me."

"Killing people isn't normal, Aiden. It's not built into us to just kill people. We are a species that thrives as a community, and killers are the oddities. The ones that don't belong. You were never meant to be the odd one out, Aiden. You were meant to grow up with a loving family. Find a girl, go to college, get a dog, and a white fence house," Danny said. At the mention of a dog, Hunter's gun dropped a little more.

"Sentimentality will get me killed," he muttered.

Danny shook his head. "A lot of people go through life being sentimental, and they normally grow old and die of natural causes."

Hunter looked around and shook his head. "I...I..."

"Just try and remember, playing in a yard with grass with a puppy smaller than yourself. That was the life you had." Danny approached him with another step. Richard was slowly lowering his gun as well.

Hunter lowered his gun and shook his head. "No, I am trained. I am made for a great purpose."

"You're not a comic book character, Aiden," Danny said gently. "You're a guy who didn't get a chance at a normal life."

Hunter shook his head. "I don't know what to do..."

"Come with me," Danny held a hand out. "Trust in

me; we'll help you, and we'll make sure you're reunited with your family."

Hunter looked down at William's corpse next to him and shook his head. "I have to finish the task... Someone has to finish the task..."

"It's no longer your task to finish," Richard's voice was soft. "There are other things in life. Things that are far better; let us show you."

Danny took another tentative step, his hand still outstretched. Hunter looked up at him with wide eyes. "I don't know what to do."

"I know, it's really confusing. You were raised to believe all these things. But we're going to help you."

Hunter sniffed and dropped his gun to the ground, slowly putting his hands above his head.

Danny reached for Hunter as Richard radioed in where they were. As Danny was about to touch Hunter's arm, a bullet passed through his head, Hunter's blood splattering over Danny's face.

The bullet had gone through the center of Hunter's forehead. Danny and Richard quickly raised their weapons and dived behind a tree each.

"It's Waters," Danny called. "I don't know how far off he is."

"He could have taken us out at any time; why take the kid out now?" Richard called.

"He was waiting to test his loyalty." Danny wiped the blood off himself, looking at Hunter's body lying next to Kitchener's. Danny peeked around the tree quickly and withdrew. Footsteps up the path let him know the backup had arrived.

"I think he's gone now," Richard said, tentatively stepping out from behind the tree. "Don't think he wanted to get caught."

Danny stepped out and knelt by Hunter before exclaiming angrily, "Goddammit!"

Richard stood beside him. "I know, he didn't deserve this life."

Danny sighed and stood up as other detectives arrived at the scene. Baker was among them.

Danny explained that Bullseye was somewhere out in the forest, probably making a getaway. A few detectives peeled off and made their way deeper into the woods.

"You're wasting your time; he's long gone," Richard told Baker. "He's not a fool."

"And the kid was?" Baker asked, looking down at Hunter's body.

Danny sighed. "A fool for trusting us, apparently. That's why Waters took him out."

Baker nodded. "At least it's over."

"It's never over when Waters is involved," Danny said, looking around. "But I will end it even if it means ending him."

Richard and Danny stayed behind while the scene was processed and the bodies were taken away. Baker approached them. "The media and the mayor will be pleased with your work. You stopped a prolific killer, Detectives."

Danny shook his head. "We stopped a misguided and probably abused kid," he said quietly. "The killer is still out there."

"I have no doubt you'll find him," Baker commented. "But having said that, there's a new division being opened in the department that I am recommending you two for."

"What new division?" Richard asked.

"It's called the SMD, the serial murders division," he explained. "There are fifty to sixty serial killers active at any given time in the country, and we certainly have our fair share. I think it's time we had people to find these guys and put them away. You two have certainly proved yourselves as having a knack for getting into these guys' heads."

Danny watched the bodies as they disappeared around a corner. "Yeah, maybe... For now, I just want to get home and shower. I'll have the report on your desk within the next two days."

Without another word, he left, leaving Richard and Baker to talk alone.

He got to his car and sat there for a moment before punching his steering wheel in frustration. After another moment, with his hand throbbing, Danny put his vehicle into reverse and left the scene, heading straight for his home.

"WHY DID FLORENTINE WANT TO SEE US?" RICHARD ASKED Danny as they pulled up to the morgue.

"I don't know," Danny commented. "He just said that we needed to get over to the morgue urgently."

They exited the car and entered the morgue. Baker was there with a few patrolmen and two other detectives. He approached them. "I think it's a warning."

"What is?" Richard asked.

"Go look for yourself," Baker said, his eyes wide.

They walked into the morgue. The fridges along the side were open, both Kitchener's and Aiden's bodies pulled out. Kitchener's was closer, and his chest was cut open. They approached cautiously, and then Richard nudged Danny. "Is that a cube?"

"It is," Florentine said from across the room. "He broke into the morgue to put it there."

"Waters..." Danny murmured.

"Clearly wanted to finish off the last masterpiece for his prodigy." Florentine approached Aiden's body.

"This was the giveaway that it was him, though." He pulled the sheet back from Aiden's body, and in the center of his forehead where the bullet had exited, there was flesh missing. The missing flesh in circles formed the perfect bullseye ring.

"I think he's pissed you cost him the lad," Florentine observed. "And I think he's going to let you know it."

Danny looked up at Florentine. "Let him come."

To Be Continued

Killer Kitteh Khristmas

Merry Meow

Jingle Fur - Coming soon

Stand Alones

The Culling

#RIPJohn

Belladonna

Buried

The Witches of Harbour

Hex

Shh...

The Priestess - Coming Soon

FANTASY TITLES

Unlikely Hero

Hidden in Plain Sight

Homeward Bound - Coming Soon

The First Hike - Coming Soon

MURDER MYSTERY TITLES

Bullseye

Stones

Animals - Coming Soon

The Seamstress - Coming Soon

GENERAL FICTION TITLES

Neutral Ground - Coming Soon

Holy Demons - Coming Soon

ABOUT THE AUTHOR

Known as the International Bestselling, Award-winning Author of horrific old-school terror titles such as Buried and the Asylum Series, Sian B. Claven brings back a nostalgic telling of creepy tales.

Aiming high, this misleadingly bubbly author terrifies her fans with tales of ghosts, murderers, and demonic possessions as though handing out candy to children, all while expanding her releases from her first young adult horror in 2017 to her more recent explicit demonic occult horror in 2021.

With an on the edge of your seat series, Claven enthralled her readers with her Butcher series, surprising them with a fourth and now final book in the series in 2021 as part of the Notorious Mind's Boxset, along with Shh, which were both part of the Soul's Day Boxset which made her an International Bestselling Author.

Claven also dabbles in the Science-Fiction Space Adventure genre, having republished her Spacehiker Adventure Series – Unlikely Hero with an updated cover and storyline after receiving criticism about the book's length. Claven looks forward to expanding this universe.

Further challenging herself, Claven also tackled writing a paranormal romance series, the first of which released as part of the Possessed by Passion boxset in March 2021. The series will continue, and Claven looks forward to exploring this new world.

Born in Southern Africa, Claven resides in Johannesburg, where she grew up with a vivid imagination and has been writing for as long as she can remember. When she was not immersing herself in books, she created her own worlds, both by herself and with her friends.

After her sister immigrated in 2017, Claven wrote and published her first book and has been on an amazing journey ever since.

Claven is an avid Harry Potter and Star Wars fan, Funko Pop Collector, 3d Puzzle builder, Diamon Art painter, and studying addict. She also has a penchant for Lego. She resides with her two best friends, their six dogs, and two cats.

Visit her website now:
www.sianbclaven.com